Wary

Torrey cleared his throat and edged closer to Sara on the bench. "I'm glad you're not in a hurry. I mean, it's hard to get to know somebody when you only see them where they work."

"I know what you mean," she replied. "It's hard enough to know what to say and how to act when you see each other at school or something."

Suddenly Torrey wasn't so sure he wanted Sara to know what he was like. What if she found out that he hung out at the Hall of Shame and that his whole life was a screwed-up mess? Warily, he said, "Maybe it won't be worth the effort to learn about me."

"No," she said, "it's *always* worth the effort to get to know somebody." Then she added, almost in a whisper, "Especially if it's somebody you already like a lot."

COUPLES

#1 *Change of Hearts*

#2 *Fire and Ice*

#3 *Alone, Together*

#4 *Made for Each Other*

#5 *Moving Too Fast*

#6 *Crazy Love*

#7 *Sworn Enemies*

#8 *Making Promises*

#9 *Broken Hearts*

#10 *Secrets*

#11 *More Than Friends*

#12 *Bad Love*

#13 *Changing Partners*

#14 *Picture Perfect*

#15 *Coming on Strong*

#16 *Sweethearts*

#17 *Dance with Me*

#18 *Kiss and Run*

#19 *Show Some Emotion*

#20 *No Contest*

#21 *Teacher's Pet*

#22 *Slow Dancing*

#23 *Bye Bye Love*

#24 *Something New*

#25 *Love Exchange*

#26 *Head Over Heels*

#27 *Sweet and Sour*

#28 *Lovestruck*

#29 *Take Me Back*

#30 *Falling for You*

#31 *Prom Date*

#32 *Playing Dirty*

#33 *Mean to Me*

#34 *Don't Get Close*

#35 *Break Away*

Special Editions
Summer Heat!
Be Mine!
Beach Party!
Sealed with a Kiss!

Coming soon . . .
#36 *Hold Me Tight*

BREAK AWAY

M.E. Cooper

SCHOLASTIC INC.
New York Toronto London Auckland Sydney

ISBN 0-590-41688-X

Copyright © 1988 by Daniel Weiss Associates, Inc. Photo: Pat Hill, copyright © 1988 Daniel Weiss Associates, Inc. All rights reserved. Published by Scholastic Inc.

12 11 10 9 8 7 6 5 4 3 2 1   8 9/8 0 1 2 3/9

Printed in the U.S.A.   01

First Scholastic printing, August 1988

BREAK AWAY

Chapter
1

"Where do you think *you're* going? I thought you'd want to hang around here until Mom and George leave for the weekend. To wave good-bye and all."

Roxanne Easton bristled at the lazily insulting tone of her brother's voice. Torrey was sprawled on the stylish sofa in the living room of the Eastons' luxurious townhouse, eating potato chips from a torn bag and drinking a soda while he leafed idly through a music magazine. Crumbs were scattered on the floor, and there was a wet ring on the surface of the coffee table where he had carelessly put his soda can.

"What business is it of yours where I go?" Roxanne asked haughtily, tossing her long, tawny hair. She put her purse down on a chair and wrinkled her nose in disgust at the crumbs. "Good grief, Tor, you are such a *slob*!"

Torrey put down his magazine and brushed a hand through his jet black hair. "It's still August, isn't it?" he asked, looking at Rox and then down at his black jeans and T-shirt. "Life in the fast lane doesn't start for another couple of weeks. So what's the big deal about how I'm dressed?"

"I didn't mean the way you look, jerk," Roxanne said scornfully. "I mean the slobby way you *act*. Look at that ring on the coffee table and those greasy potato chips all over the floor. George is going to explode when he sees this place."

"Who cares about George?" The corner of Torrey's lip curled. "He can scream all he wants, it doesn't matter to me." He picked up his magazine again, then looked up at Roxanne with a lazy grin. He ain't *my* boss. He can't fire *me*."

Roxanne began to fume. Unfortunately Torrey was right. The George they were talking about was George Royce, her mother's boyfriend, who was also the owner of the Foxy Lady, a designer clothing and beachwear shop. Roxanne had worked there for most of the summer, until she quit to go to leadership camp. Ever since George had started dating her mother, he'd declared himself a father figure for Roxanne and Torrey. By itself, maybe, that wouldn't have been so bad. After all, since their parents' divorce, they only saw their real father when their mother wanted to get rid of them for a week or two. No, the trouble was more the way George *acted*. He was always telling them what to do and what to wear.

2

The next thing Rox and Torrey knew, he'd probably be telling them who their friends ought to be. Then there'd *really* be trouble. Roxanne already disliked him, but if he didn't start minding his own business, things were bound to get worse.

"Anyway," Torrey went on, turning the page of his magazine, "you haven't answered my question. Where are you going?"

"I might've answered if you'd asked in a nicer tone," Roxanne muttered. She gave her makeup a quick inspection in the mirror over the buffet, smiling a little at her reflection. Her red hair hung loose around her shoulders and her skin — finally free of the poison ivy that had been such torment — was still a golden tan. The emerald blouse she was wearing made her eyes look even greener. "I'm going to the Saturday Market with Charlotte." She added, "That is if I can get the car." She glanced down at the tray where her mother always tossed the keys to the Jaguar. Good, they were there. Fortunately, Mrs. Easton's *newest* car (the third this year) was an automatic, and she could drive it herself without being chauffered around. Now all Roxanne had to do was convince her mother to give her the keys.

Torrey sat up. "Hey, wait a minute," he said, glaring at his sister. "It's *my* turn to have the car. I'm going over to the Hall of Fame this afternoon to meet some of the guys. There's a new band auditioning, and we want to hear it."

Roxanne let out a short laugh. "The Hall of *Shame* — *that* sleazy place? The car'll be stripped clean in five minutes if you park it outside that

3

sewage dump. Anyway, the last time I got the car was when I had to see the doctor about my ankle, and that doesn't count. Besides, I *have* to have the car today. It's a matter of life and death."

This time, Roxanne told herself grimly, she wasn't exaggerating. She hadn't seen Vince DiMase since leadership camp, and if she didn't see him today at the Saturday Market, she probably *would* die. She'd counted so much on being able to win him back during the week they'd spent at camp, but all her efforts had ended in miserable failure.

The only things she'd gotten out of leadership camp were a twisted ankle and a terrible case of poison ivy. As a result, she'd had to stay cooped up so nobody could see her for a while. Now she was better, though, and she absolutely *had* to see Vince.

"So who cares whether you live or die?" Torrey asked hatefully. He tossed the magazine over the back of the sofa and added in an even tone, "It's my turn to take the car, and I'm taking it."

"Oh, no, you're not!" Roxanne shouted, stamping her foot. "I'm going to the Market with Charlotte, and you can't stop me!"

At that moment, George Royce came into the living room and gave Roxanne a stern look. He was a distinguished-looking man, dressed in neat slacks and an expensive-looking open-collared shirt. "What's going on in here?" he asked sharply, smoothing back his graying hair. "What's all the yelling about? I could hear you two all the

4

way down the hall." He stared at them with a look of disgust. "Is that all you kids ever do — bicker?" He glanced at the mess they'd made. "And just look at this place. Your mother paid a decorator a lot of money to redo this room, and you've completely trashed it."

"Is that you, George?" Jodi Easton called in a sugary tone from the top of the stairs. "I'm almost finished packing. I'll be with you in a minute."

"Mom," Roxanne cried, going over to the stairs, "tell Torrey that I'm taking the car so Charlotte and I can go to the Saturday Market."

"No, Mom!" Torrey yelled after her. "Tell Roxanne that it's *my* turn. She took the car the last time."

"Oh, Rox, Torrey," Mrs. Easton said with a weary sigh, "can't you settle this little squabble yourselves? I've got so much to do before I leave."

Inside, Roxanne could feel the anger beginning to well up. That was the way her mother always acted. She would never take a stand, one way or the other. It didn't matter *how* obnoxious Torrey was, or how disgracefully he behaved with those punk friends of his. Her mother never disciplined him. She was simply indifferent to everything that happened. Sometimes it was enough to make Roxanne want to go out and do something really *awful*, something that — just for once — would get her mother's attention. But when she really stopped to think about it, she got the despairing feeling that no matter what she did, her mother would barely notice. It was a lost cause.

5

"Never mind, Jodi," George Royce said, raising his voice, "I can take care of this little problem. You go on and get ready." He turned to Torrey. "Now," he began in a fatherly, let's-be-reasonable tone, "what's this dispute about, Torrey?"

Torrey shrugged. "Nothing," he said sullenly, obviously unwilling to help George play self-appointed disciplinarian. Roxanne could sympathize with her brother on that score, anyway. George was only their mother's boyfriend, the most recent in a long string of them. He had no right to act like their father.

George turned to Roxanne. "Perhaps *you* can tell me, young lady," he said, scowling, "just what is going on here? Shouldn't you be down at the shop?"

Roxanne cleared her throat. Maybe she could get what she wanted if she pulled her poor-little-me act. "You know why I'm not at work anymore," she said in the most mournful tone she could manage. "After leadership camp and being cooped up with poison ivy for the last couple of weeks, I've lost so much time this summer. Today is the first day I've felt well enough to go out, and I wanted to spend it with my friends. Is that so awful?" She gave George the pouting smile that usually won people — especially *males* — over. "After all, school starts soon, and then I won't have *any* free time, especially if I work every Saturday at the shop."

Roxanne fixed her gaze on George, silently urging him to say yes.

"Well," he began in a deliberate tone, "if it's Torrey's turn to have the car, he ought to have it." His face took on a sterner look. "And it's an indisputable fact, isn't it, Roxanne, that you are not the most careful of drivers. There's the little matter of that stop sign you ran last month. Remember?"

Roxanne snorted. George had recently caught her coasting through the stop sign at the end of their street. Roxanne's driving record was clean — she'd never gotten so much as a parking ticket — but ever since then, he'd been nagging about her careless driving. As if he had the right to tell her how she should drive! Really, George was a major pain.

And now it wasn't just George. Torrey was getting in on the act, too. "Yeah, what about that, Rox?" he asked wickedly. "Don't forget about that stop sign."

Suddenly Roxanne's anger — at Torrey, at her mother, at George — boiled over in a burst of uncontrollable fury. "Stop sign?" she shouted, slamming her fist down on the buffet so hard that the keys rattled in the dish. "Don't you talk to me about *stop signs*, Torrey Easton! Not when you *totaled* Mom's Mercedes!"

There was silence in the room. Then George coughed. "She's right, Torrey," he said. "You have no right to talk to your sister like that. That accident of yours was inexcusable."

A dull red flush crept up Torrey's cheeks, and Roxanne saw a look of sheer hatred in his eyes. She also saw something else — some kind of resignation. But then he lowered his eyes, and all she could see was the angry twist to his mouth. "That was months ago," he said in a bored voice.

"It was not," Roxanne pointed out smugly. "It was only the beginning of summer. Surely you haven't forgotten it so quickly." She glanced at George to make sure her words were having the desired effect. Slyly, she added, "And as far as I know, you've hardly been punished."

Torrey *had* been driving their mother's Mercedes when they'd had the wreck in June. He'd been racing like a madman and lost control of the car. They'd spun around and landed in a ditch. Luckily, Rox and Torrey were unhurt, but the car was totaled. And when Vince showed up with the Rose Hill Volunteer Rescue Squad, Roxanne had seen her chance to save her skin.

She'd burst into hysterical tears. *She'd* been driving, she told Vince. She'd wrecked the car because she was so distraught over the fact that he'd stood her up. Torrey told the truth to the police and to their mother, of course, but Rox let Vince believe her lie — especially after seeing how well it had worked. Always the wonderful, chivalrous knight, Vince was so touched by her distress and her tears that he took her in his arms and apologized profusely. Roxanne sighed. Of course, back then she'd only been using Vince to get in with the crowd. She hadn't been in love with him then. Not until later, at his family's picnic on the Fourth of July, had Rox realized that Vince truly was the right boy for her.

"You were never punished?" George asked

sternly, breaking into Roxanne's thoughts. Two deep creases appeared on his forehead, and he frowned at Torrey. "I thought your mother was going to take care of that."

Roxanne tilted her head. "Sometimes Mother forgets," she said sweetly. Torrey flashed her a pleading look, but she ignored it. "I guess this was one of those times."

"I see," George said. He raised his voice. "Jodi, could you come down here, please? There's something I have to ask you about."

Mrs. Easton came down the stairs, looking cool and elegant in white silk pants and a shimmery pink blouse, her blonde hair carefully coiffed. "Can't this wait, George?" she asked. "The Wilsons expect us for lunch at one, and it's a two-hour drive out to the country. We're *already* late."

"No, it *can't* wait," George insisted. "We've got to get to the bottom of this right away. Roxanne says that Torrey was never punished for wrecking the car. Is that right?"

Jodi Easton sighed and crossed the room. Standing beside Roxanne, she regarded herself in the mirror, patting her hair. "Oh, I'm sure I punished him," she said. "I don't know if it was official or not." She turned to face Torrey. "Didn't I tell you that you couldn't drive the new car for a week, Torrey?"

"A *week*?" George exploded. "For heaven's sake, Jodi, where's your sense of discipline? Your son wrecked your brand-new car — he was racing it, no less! And now you're allowing him to drive

9

the Jaguar. How long will it take for him to trash this one? Torrey should have been grounded for the entire summer! If you don't take a firm stand on things like this, how can you expect him to have any respect for you or your rules? Why, if you keep this up, the next thing you know, he'll be *stealing* cars instead of racing them. You've got to show him who's the boss."

Torrey darted a final pleading glance toward Roxanne, who answered him with a slight shrug of her shoulders. Why should she care what happened to her brother? He didn't care anything about her. Anyway, George looked mad enough to punish Torrey himself, which meant that she was sure to get the car today. Torrey might even get grounded for a month or two, Rox thought happily. If that happened, she'd have exclusive rights to the car. She smiled a triumphant little smile and glanced down at the car keys. Yes indeed, this was going to work out after all, almost as well as if she'd planned it herself.

"Do we have to deal with this right now, George?" Mrs. Easton asked with a sigh. "After all, we *are* late, and — "

"We certainly *do* have to deal with it now!" George said angrily. He looked as if he were going to blow up. "If you're not willing to take a stern hand with your son, *I* am! When I'm through with him, he'll know who's running things around here!"

Roxanne took a deep breath. She wanted Torrey to be punished, to get him out of her way, but she also hated to see Geoge dealing himself into the family again. Where had he gotten the idea that he could do *anything* to either of them? And why didn't her mother step in and take charge of the situation, the way a mother *ought* to?

Mrs. Easton looked at Torrey indecisively. "Well, I don't know . . ." she said. "I'm not sure what to do. After all, the insurance company has already taken care of the car, and. . . . "

Roxanne let out her breath in an impatient sigh. Her mother would *never* change. She would just let things drift on the way they were forever. And meanwhile there was George, giving orders and acting like he was their father.

"Fine. I'll handle it," George said. He wheeled around to face Torrey, his face set and angry. "Young man, you've been a trial to your mother ever since I've known you. You're lazy and thoughtless and you have no sense of responsibility. So I'm laying down the law. You're not to touch that car for two months. What's more, you're not even to *ride* in it, except when your mother's driving, so you can forget about begging your sister to drive you around."

Roxanne could hear Torrey's gasp all the way across the room. "Two months!" he protested. "But school is starting pretty soon! And I've already got tickets to the Iron Alloy concert next week in D.C.! How am I going to get there without — "

"I don't care how you get to the concert. As for school, you can take the bus. And if you get tired of that, you can always ride that five-hundred-dollar racing bike your father bought you last Christmas. It won't hurt you to get some exercise."

Roxanne could see her brother breathing hard, fighting the impulse to let George have it. "You don't have any right to tell me what to do," he said lamely. Torrey turned to his mother. "Mom, tell him that he can't order us around like this! It's not fair!"

Jodi Easton cleared her throat, her eyes darting from Torrey to George. "Maybe two months is a little harsh," she began in a hesitant tone.

"Don't you see!" George said. He went over and put his hands on her shoulders. "If you don't make Torrey toe the line now, there's no telling where he'll go wrong in the future."

Jodi sighed. "I suppose you're right, George."

George reached into the tray and picked up the keys to the Jaguar. He turned to Roxanne. "Do you think you can behave like a responsible adult if you're allowed to use the car?"

"Yes, sir," Roxanne said meekly, her eyes on the keyring dangling in George's fingers like a tantalizing silver talisman. Keys to freedom. Keys to a fantastic Saturday of fun in the Market with Charlotte and the possibility of a wonderful reunion with Vince.

"You two have to grow up and learn to act like civilized human beings," George went on pompously. He was still holding the keys just out of Roxanne's reach, looking as if he was enjoying himself. "Growing up is painful, but it's something we all have to face. Self-discipline and

12

responsibility are important elements of being an adult."

Roxanne nodded, her muscles tensed. Get to the point, George, she urged silently. Am I going to get the car or not?

"So even though I'm not entirely convinced that you'll act responsibly, I'm going to let you have the Jaguar for the weekend, Roxanne. I believe children ought to have the chance to prove they can conduct themselves properly. Just don't get into any trouble with it, okay?"

Roxanne nodded again. The entire weekend! That was even better than she'd hoped. She cast a triumphant glance at Torrey, who was standing with his head down, viciously digging the toe of his shoe into the plush carpet, obviously smoldering with anger. Maybe she ought to feel sorry for her brother, but she couldn't. All she could feel was the triumph of having gotten what she wanted. She reached for the keys and tucked them safely into her purse.

"I won't get into any kind of trouble at all," she promised.

Chapter 2

Seething with anger over George's lecture, Torrey wheeled his dusty bike out of the garage and climbed on to the leather seat. It was a Peugeot, a top-of-the-line racing bike. Torrey's father always made sure that his son got super-expensive presents, even if his secretary was the one who actually bought them, but Torrey had only ridden it a couple of times. As far as he was concerned, riding a bike around Rose Hill was the height of dorkdom, especially when there was a sleek, high-powered Jag sitting in the garage just begging to be let loose. Torrey pedaled down the drive and coasted into the street, swerving to miss a car coming around the corner. It would serve George right if he got wiped out on his stupid bike.

Torrey snorted. Good old George. *He* was becoming a major problem. Before George came on the scene, Torrey could practically blow up the place and his mom wouldn't even notice. But George thought he owned the entire Easton family. He complained about the stereo and nagged about picking up the living room. He'd even talked to their mother once or twice about putting Torrey and Rox on an allowance, instead of letting them just ask for money whenever they needed any. It was ridiculous the way that man had taken over.

Torrey stopped at a nearby minimart and bought a couple of candy bars, stuffing one in his mouth and one into his pocket as he got back on the bike and bounced off the curb. Of course, George was only temporary, Torrey reasoned. Pretty soon his mother would get bored and tell him to take a walk.

No, Roxanne was the only one Torrey was *really* angry about. Like all girls, she was a manipulator through and through. You could never trust her. No matter how sweet she talked or how beautiful and innocent she looked, she'd get you in the end. Roxanne was worse than George, but his mother was the most despicable for letting everyone push her around.

Torrey coasted around the corner. Ahead of him was Kennedy High, where school would start again in a couple of weeks. The thought of school made him even sicker. Roxanne and her crowd were all pumped up about school starting and football games and the school paper and homecoming, but Torrey couldn't stand any of that rah-rah garbage. As far as he was concerned, it was just plain stupid to get so heated up about stuff like that. It was all so boring, so meaningless, such a stupid waste of time. He grinned — his friends weren't interested in school stuff, either. Like him, they were more into hanging out and listening to good, heavy music, like the band that was going to audition at the Hall of Fame this afternoon. At the thought of the Hall of Fame — the Hall of Shame, as it was called — his spirits began to rise. That was where he belonged, listening to music, playing video games with his friends, maybe dancing a little. That was where he could forget what a stupid, boring place the world really was and how empty he felt when he thought about the future. Yeah, the Hall of Shame was more like home than home was.

The traffic was heavier now, and Torrey began to pump faster, weaving in and out between the cars. He ran a red light and turned the corner to take a one-way street — the wrong way — as a short cut, startling a couple of motorists who had to frantically slam on their brakes to avoid him. He grinned to himself as he did a wheelie onto a curb and barely missed a little old man with a stupid poodle. The old man shook his fist as Torrey flew past. Maybe this bike stuff wasn't so bad after all. Taking chances, taking risks, getting people to notice him — *that* was what made him feel alive, what helped him to forget how meaningless his life was. That was the thing about racing his mother's Mercedes — it made him feel alive, it gave him a jolt, it excited him. Sometimes being scared was a heck of a lot better than doing

16

nothing and letting the emptiness inside eat you up.

Torrey glanced at his watch as he biked into the minimall where the Hall of Fame was located. Good, he wasn't going to be late after all. But as he locked up the bike, he looked over at the club's entrance. A CLOSED sign hung on the door, and a big piece of plywood had been nailed over the front window. The manager was just coming out, closing the door behind him and locking it.

"Hey, man," Torrey said, "what's going on? How come you're closing up? What happened to the audition that was scheduled for this afternoon?"

"The audition's been scrubbed," the manager said. "We're closed for repairs." He looked angry.

"Repairs?" Torrey said blankly. Then he nodded. "Oh, yeah, you mean that little bust-up last night." After the rock group had finished playing the night before, their fans had gone wild, breaking up the furniture, tearing down a couple of doors, breaking the big window in front. Torrey had stayed on the sidelines, but even he had been a little surprised at the amount of damage the kids had done before the cops showed up.

"The repairs for that 'little bust-up,' as you call it," the manager said bitterly, "have put us out of business for a couple of weeks. And what's more, the town says that if you kids don't cool down, we might have to close *permanently*." He pocketed his keys and strode off, leaving Torrey staring after him with his mouth open.

Closed? The Hall of Shame was *closed*? Torrey's shoulders slumped. What was he going to do *now*? Where was he going to go at night? He went back to get his bike and then wandered listlessly around the mall, dragging it with him as he looked into windows. Nothing caught his interest. He'd already seen the movie that was playing at the Cineplex, and he couldn't think of anything to buy. Finally, unable to shake his growing depression, he parked the bike in front of the Video Stop and went in. Maybe he'd rent a couple of movies. With his mom and George gone for the weekend and Roxanne out for who knew how long, there was nobody to tell him what to do. He could zone out watching movies all afternoon.

But even though he wandered around the aisles for ten or fifteen minutes, pulling down video cartons and reading their blurbs, he still couldn't find a movie he wanted to see. Everything looked so dull, so boring. All the movies were either sappy love stories or adventure flicks that were practically cartoons. None of them seemed *real*.

Then, out of the corner of his eye, he saw a girl. She'd just gotten up from a typewriter behind the counter, and she was tacking a typed sheet to one of the video shelves. She was cute, an all-American blonde, with long, thick hair and rosy cheeks. She was wearing a loose-fitting man's shirt and trim khaki shorts, with knee socks and sneakers, and her large tortoiseshell glasses gave her a look of brainy seriousness. For a minute or two, Torrey watched her as she snapped another sheet of paper into the typewriter and bent over the keys, her hair falling in a graceful wave across her face. Yeah, she was cute all right. Torrey straightened his shoulders and ran a hand through his dark hair. Maybe he would go over and say hi to her. But then he sighed and turned away, shoving his hands into the pockets of his jeans. Aw, who cared? He didn't feel like going to any trouble. Anyway, she looked pretty straight. Chances were she wouldn't go for somebody like him. He'd learned that lesson from Katie Crawford — one of those stuck-up "crowd" kids who had hung out with Torrey for a while, having fun and raising a little hell. But she was just doing it for attention, to get back at her sappy boyfriend Greg. Torrey walked down another aisle, aimlessly looking at videos.

"Can I help you find something?"

Torrey looked up. The girl was coming toward him. Up close, she was even prettier than she had seemed from a distance. Her blonde hair was streaked with taffy-colored highlights, and her smile lit up her face, making her blue eyes sparkle. On any other day, he would have been more interested. But not today. Today he was feeling too listless to even make the effort.

"No, I'm just looking," Torrey said dully. He turned away.

"Well, if you can't make up your mind, maybe you'd like to take a look at some of my movie reviews," the girl suggested, following him down the aisle. "I've been putting them on the shelves with all our recent releases — and a lot of older movies too."

"Movie reviews?" Torrey asked, curious in

spite of himself. So that was what she'd been typing.

The girl nodded, her blue eyes dancing. "Yes. I've noticed that people hate to take a chance on a movie they don't know anything about, so I decided to post quick rundowns of the plots and characters. It helps the customers decide which movie to rent, and it's fun for me. I *love* writing about the movies."

Torrey leaned against the shelf and crossed his arms, regarding the girl with growing interest. There was something about her smile, about the way she tossed her heavy blonde hair, that made him want to know more about her. He cleared his throat. "I guess you'd have to know a lot about movies to be able to write reviews, wouldn't you?" he asked. He wasn't especially interested in movies, but *she* obviously was.

The girl smiled modestly, "Well, I've been studying films for a long time." She waved her hand. "I can tell you about almost every video in the store. I live and *breathe* movies. When I go to college I'm going to study film. Maybe I'll be a reviewer for real some day. Or maybe I'll get involved in filmmaking."

Torrey leaned forward, catching a scent of the girl's fresh perfume, admiring the way the light shimmered in her hair. Maybe it *was* worth the bother, after all. "Is that all you do," he asked with a half smile. "Watch movies?"

The girl didn't answer immediately. Instead, she was studying him with a slightly puzzled look.

Then she said, "Hey, don't I know you? Weren't we in the same English class at Kennedy last spring? Aren't you Torrey Easton?"

Torrey nodded. That was funny — he didn't remember seeing her before. But then, he reasoned, he'd always been so uninspired by English that he rarely paid any attention to anything — or anybody — in the class. In fact, he'd cultivated the habit of not paying attention to the point where he sometimes wondered if he could concentrate if he had to. "Yeah, I'm Torrey," he finally said. "What's your name?"

"Sara Gates," the girl replied. She leaned forward, looking eagerly at him. "Sure, I remember now. Ms. Kean was always bugging you about turning in your assignments late." She smiled a little reminiscently. "It's kind of strange that I didn't recognize you right away. I always got this hostile feeling from you, like you felt like you were in the wrong place at the wrong time or something. Like you really didn't enjoy being in school."

Torrey stepped back, bristling. The last thing he needed right now was to be reminded of his continual failures. Who did this girl think she was, anyway, some kind of psychoanalyst? "Yeah, well, what's so strange about not liking school?" he growled, feeling a burst of anger. "And you've got it right. I'm not interested in school. And I'm not interested in dumb movies, either — with or without reviews." With that he turned on his heel and walked out.

Sara swallowed hard as she watched Torrey stalk out the door and begin unlocking an expensive-looking racing bike chained to the rack out front. Why did she always have to open her big mouth? No wonder he'd run off after what she said about English class, Sara thought. And now she'd wasted a perfect chance to get to know him! She'd had her eye on Torrey all semester, even though he never noticed her — or anyone else, for that matter. It wasn't just his rugged good looks that had attracted her, either. It was something else, something deeper. Most of the other kids hung around in groups of friends, but Torrey Easton was a real loner. Once or twice, when she looked at him, she'd seen a lost look in his eyes, a kind of restless, searching sadness. She even looked for him at school activities, wondering what he did when he wasn't in class. But he was never at any of the dances or pep rallies or anything like that. After a while, she'd given up. Today, she saw that same lost look in his eyes that she'd recognized before, and a kind of sad remoteness, too, as if nothing mattered to him.

Suddenly, impulsively, Sara pulled a video off the shelf and dashed toward the door. Torrey was just getting on his bike. "Torrey, wait!" she called.

Torrey looked back over his shoulder. "What do you want?" he growled.

"I just thought of a movie I'm sure you'll like," Sara said breathlessly. "*Breaking Away*. If you're into biking, you just *have* to see it. It's about these four guys, sort of misfits, who hang around together. But this one guy is into bikes, and they wind up having this big bicycle race and — "

But Torrey stopped her in midsentence. "Okay, okay, I'll take it," he said in an impatient tone, pulling the video out of her fingers.

Sara stared at him, surprised.

Torrey began to pedal away. "Put it on my mom's charge," he yelled over his shoulder.

Sara stared as Torrey darted out into the traffic. She was still standing in front of the video store, still watching him, when he glanced back at her. Then he pedaled furiously away.

Chapter
3

Roxanne pulled up in front of Charlotte DeVries's large, white-columned house just in time to see Charlotte come out of the front door and pause on the steps. Roxanne honked once, and Charlotte turned to wave to her mother, who was standing in the doorway.

"See you tonight," she called, in her charming southern drawl. "I won't be late." Then she came toward Roxanne, her full skirt swishing around her.

Roxanne couldn't help smiling. Standing outlined against the house's white columns, with her pink sundress and long blonde hair, Charlotte DeVries looked every inch the southern belle she was. Sweet and demure. She was full of a soft charm that made people want to be her friend. But Charlotte could also be firm and decisive when she had to be. And what's more, she was popular with the crowd. That was a point that had always counted heavily with Roxanne. Her friendship with Frankie Baker had been rewarding in many ways, mostly because Frankie had been so anxious to please her. But it had also been kind of a drag to hang around with somebody who wasn't very popular. Charlotte, however, was different. Charlotte was a real leader, and everybody admired her for it. Including Roxanne.

"Hi, there," Charlotte said, sliding onto the rich leather of the front seat. "It seems like *months* since I've seen you! How are you feeling — better?" Her blue eyes mirrored the genuine concern that filled her voice.

Basking in Charlotte's sympathy, Roxanne glanced at herself in the mirror. "The poison ivy's all gone," she said. "Thank goodness. You can't imagine how long the two weeks were, all alone in that house. I looked so horrible — all red and puffed up." She shuddered. "I can't imagine how *you* could bear to visit me. Of course, I couldn't see Vince and I didn't dare call him. If he didn't hate me before, I'm sure he does now. Knowing that made it even more terrible."

"Oh, you poor thing," Charlotte said, patting Roxanne's hand. "But the important thing is that you're all better and that we're going to celebrate by having fun at the Market! Maybe Vince will even be there. He doesn't hate you, you know. He may just need some time, that's all. He'll probably come around. Anyway," she added in a more matter-of-fact tone, "I saw Karen Davis at the drugstore last night, and she told me that the whole crowd is planning to show up."

"I hope so," Roxanne said, starting the engine. "After the morning I've had with Torrey and Mom and George, I really need a day of fun and friends."

"Trouble at home?" Charlotte asked in a tentative voice.

Roxanne nodded. "It's so hard sometimes, Charlotte," she said, letting her voice break, hoping for even more sympathy. "Torrey and George and I got into a big fight over the car and the wreck this summer and — "

She stopped abruptly. Even though Charlotte was now her closest friend, Roxanne hadn't told any of her friends that she'd lied to Vince about who was driving the Mercedes when the wreck happened — not even Charlotte. In fact, she'd only told Charlotte bits and pieces about her relationship with Vince and about the things she'd done to try to get him back again. She hadn't told the whole truth because it seemed to put her in such a bad light. It made her seem thoughtless and selfish when she wasn't that way at all. And since she hadn't told Charlotte the truth in the beginning, it wasn't really possible to tell her now.

"I understand how you must feel," Charlotte said, ignoring the awkward silence. "But try to forget about all that stuff and have some fun. You deserve it."

Roxanne nodded. Charlotte was right. After

what she'd been through, she *did* deserve to have some fun. And fun was exactly what she was going to have!

The Saturday Market, a combination crafts fair, flea market, and bake sale, was taking place in the older section of Rose Hill, near the skating rink and the railroad tracks. The shaded, three-acre site was crowded with weathered wooden booths set up in long rows. Loud-voiced vendors hawked chili dogs and pizza, thick wedges of warm apple pie and homemade ice cream, and Roxanne could smell the buttery aroma of popcorn wafting through the air. The PA system was playing a country-western tune, and everybody looked as if they were having a great time.

"Oh, look," Charlotte said, pointing to a small booth. "Just *look* at all those wonderful hats!" The front of the booth was covered with wide straw hats adorned with flowers and lacy ribbons. "I just have to have that white one with the pink flowers and ribbons," she said. "It'll be perfect to keep the sun out of my eyes."

"I think I'll stick to sunglasses," Roxanne said with a laugh. "Ribbons and lace aren't exactly my style." She laughed to herself at the way she used to dress for Vince — real natural-looking, with just a little makeup. Roxanne learned quickly, though. Today she wore a hot-pink-and-purple crop-top, with purple leggings and hot-pink flats. Oddly enough, one of the things that seemed to impress Vince was her flamboyant fashion sense; it intrigued him.

After Charlotte had paid for her hat and Roxanne had bought a couple of pink and purple balloons, the girls began to walk around, with Charlotte oohing and aahing over the homespun crafts and Roxanne searching the crowd impatiently for any sign of Vince. She just *had* to see him today! Their breakup had seemed so final, and she hadn't been able to change his mind during the week they'd spent at leadership camp. But she couldn't give up hope. Surely, if she explained everything and apologized, told him over and over that she knew she'd been wrong, he would understand. He *had* to understand!

The girls wandered through the Market, chatting idly about their friends, about school, and about all the crazy things that had happened that summer — especially leadership camp. That was where Charlotte and Roxanne had really gotten to know one another for the first time.

"Oh, that reminds me," Charlotte said, snapping her fingers. "What're you going to give your speech on at the meeting next week?"

Roxanne stared at her with a blank look on her face. "Speech? What speech? And what meeting? What are you talking about?"

"Didn't you get the notice?" Charlotte replied, picking up a straw basket and looking at it. "Mine came in the mail a couple of days ago. You should have gotten yours by now."

Roxanne stared at her. "Notice? What notice?"

"From the Rotary Club." When Roxanne didn't reply, Charlotte put the basket down. "Well, maybe it went to Jana Lacey instead."

Jana had originally been chosen for leadership camp, but at the last minute she'd gone to England on a student exchange, and Roxanne had taken her place. "That's probably just what happened. Anyway, the Rotary Club — you know, the people who helped sponsor the camp — is having this big meeting at the Holiday Inn. All the kids who went to leadership camp — you, me, Vince, and Daniel — are supposed to give a speech about their experiences."

Roxanne hooted. "Me? Give a speech? You've got to be kidding! They'll never get *me* up there in front of all those old men."

Charlotte looked at her curiously. "But why not? You're not shy, Rox, and I know you like to talk. And anyway, it's not just going to be the Rotary Club. Kennedy students are invited, too. There'll be lots of people there — people we know — from all over the area." She smiled with encouragement. "It really should be fun."

Roxanne made a face. "Fun for you, maybe. Sure, I like to talk to my friends, and I'm not a bit shy when it comes to meeting people, especially guys. But I'm just not cut out for public speaking, that's all there is to it. There's no way that I'm going to give a speech." She shuddered. "Just the thought of it gives me cold chills up and down my spine."

Charlotte grabbed her arm. "Hey, look," she broke in excitedly, "it's Jonathan and Lily!" she began to wave. "Hi, Lily! Hi, Jonathan!"

Lily Rorshak, blonde and waifish, danced toward them, holding a huge, dark brown teddy

29

bear. "Look what Jonathan bought me," she announced, finishing up a waltz. "A dancing partner."

Jonathan Preston, former student activities director at Kennedy High, grinned as he draped an arm around Lily's slender shoulders. *"Someone's* got to take care of her while I'm away at Penn," he said lazily, pushing the brim of his Indiana Jones fedora back with his index finger. Then he whispered loudly out of the corner of his mouth, "The bear is bugged! I'll know her every movement!"

Lily giggled and shook her head. "The real question, Jonathan, is who's going to keep an eye on *you*? Who's going to keep *you* out of trouble?" Jonathan had a reputation among his friends for sometimes being a little crazy and unpredictable. It was one of the things Lily loved most about him.

"Trouble? What trouble?" It was Daniel Tackett, with Greg Montgomery close behind him. Daniel pushed his longish brown hair out of his eyes and looked around, grinning. "Is somebody in trouble?"

Roxanne laughed. "No more than usual, Daniel," she said, trying to warm up to him. Daniel was from Stevenson High, too, and knew all about Roxanne's sordid past. She still wasn't on the firmest ground with the crowd, but they all seemed to really like Daniel, so Roxanne was trying her hardest to be cordial to him. Connections; that was the name of the game. Daniel had been appointed editor in chief of *The Red and the*

Gold for next year, and it was definitely worth charming him.

Roxanne, on the other hand, had not truly been accepted until recently, after she started going out with Vince DiMase. And she still wasn't sure that the crowd really liked and trusted her. She had the uneasy feeling that if she did something even the slightest bit wrong, she'd find herself on the outside again in a big hurry. Today, feeling so uncertain about Vince — and her position in the crowd — she felt grateful there were a lot of people around.

Daniel grinned at her. "Well, well, if it isn't our dear Roxanne," he teased, "back after a short detour into the poison ivy patch." He pulled out an imaginary notebook and pencil and began to take notes like a newspaper reporter. "Tell me, how do you feel now that you're back in action?"

"Well. . . . " Roxanne hesitated. The others weren't listening, and she really wanted to ask Daniel whether Vince was coming to the Market today, but she couldn't think of a way to do it without calling attention to the question. Finally she just shrugged and turned toward Jonathan and Lily, who were telling Charlotte something that sounded important.

At that moment, Karen Davis and Brian Pierson wandered up, their arms around each other. Karen and Brian were both headed for Brown University that fall. Frankie Baker and Josh Ferguson were with them, and Josh was wearing a pair of denim overalls and a green T-shirt, with a straw hat mashed down over his ears. Frankie was carrying a bag of used books she'd bought at one of the flea market stalls.

"Hi, Charlotte," Karen said warmly. "How are you?" She glanced at Roxanne — not a very warm glance, Roxanne thought. After Rox had started going with Vince, the rest of the crowd had seemed to accept her, but not Karen. "We haven't seen much of you for the last few weeks," she observed dryly.

"Oh, I was away at leadership camp," Roxanne said, wanting to remind Karen that she'd been one of the four Kennedy students to go that year. Of course, Roxanne wasn't exactly *chosen* to attend, but she looked around to see whether the others were listening anyway. Lily was talking to Charlotte, but Daniel and Brian and Jonathan were watching her. "The camp was *terrific*, wasn't it, Daniel?" she asked, raising her voice a little so everybody would hear. "I think it's really going to help us lead the school this year."

Of course, Charlotte, Vince, and Daniel already *had* positions of leadership — Vince was president of Wilderness Club, Daniel had the newspaper, and Charlotte had taken Jonathan's job as student activities director. But before long, everybody would recognize *her* potential, too. It was just a matter of time, Roxanne assured herself. She pretended not to see Karen's raised eyebrows.

Daniel nodded. "Yeah, it was terrific, all right," he said. He turned to Greg. "You really missed a great experience." Seeing the disappointed look on his friend's face, Daniel added, "But seeing Katie off was more important. So, uh, does she like Florida?"

Greg's eyes clouded over. His girlfriend, Katie Crawford, had been asked to start at the University of Florida early, and she'd been gone for three weeks already.

"Yeah. She's getting settled in, and she really likes it a lot," Greg said. "But I can tell you one thing, a long-distance romance sure eats up the money. We've been talking on the phone a couple of times a week."

Josh laughed. "I believe it," he said. "It's not going to get any better when school starts, either. There'll be so much more to tell her about — classes, dances, football games . . ."

"I'm glad to see you're all discussing football," came a deep voice. Roxanne looked around and saw hunky Zack McGraw walk up with his girlfriend, Stacy Morrison, who was one of Kennedy's most promising gymnasts. "After all, the season starts in a few short weeks. The coach has us doing two-a-days already, and we're getting psyched up for that first game."

"So how come you're here at the Market and not on the football field?" Lily asked.

"Time off for good behavior," Zack replied innocently, and everybody laughed. "I can't wait for that first game, though," he said, tightening his fists. "We're going to steamroll 'em!"

"Speaking of steamrollers," Josh said, "has anybody else got Mitchell for English this term?"

Everybody laughed.

"Maybe it won't be so bad," Stacy said, her voice sympathetic. "Anyway, school is two whole weeks away. We've got lots of time before we hit the books."

"Hey, I have a great idea," Charlotte announced enthusiastically. "Is anybody interested in going to the state fair?"

"Yeah, the Maryland State Fair starts next week," said Josh.

"Oh, that sounds like fun, Char," Roxanne agreed quickly. Vince would certainly be there. And anyway, an outing would give her another opportunity to solidify her position with the crowd.

"We could go the day before school starts," Charlotte told them. It's a Sunday, so hopefully no one will have to work, and it will give us a chance to get together before we have to start thinking about classes again."

Jonathan nudged Karen. "See, I told you we made the right choice," he said. "The new student activities director's already directing. We're leaving the crowd in good hands, wouldn't you say?"

"I say that Charlotte's idea has a lot of promise," Greg said. "Maryland State Fair, here we come."

Some of them began to chat excitedly about the fair as others said good-bye and turned to leave. Daniel came over to Charlotte and Roxanne. "Have you started working on your speeches yet?" he asked.

Charlotte frowned. "Well, I've been trying to

think of a topic, but I haven't come up with anything yet. Have you?"

Daniel nodded, his brown eyes intent. "Yeah. I'm going to talk about my plans for the newspaper this year. It'll be a good chance to let some of the big-business types in Rose Hill know that the student paper isn't just a gag-rag and that they ought to take it seriously. Who knows? I may even be able to drum up some new advertising business. And Vince has decided to speak about his volunteer work with the Rose Hill Volunteer Rescue Squad."

"It sounds like you guys are really giving this a lot of thought," Charlotte said.

Daniel nodded. "Sure we are. Both of us think of this meeting as our chance to let the city fathers know that the younger generation doesn't spend *all* its time hanging out and having a good time. In fact, the two of us are getting together tomorrow to work on our speeches — you know, help each other out." He glanced at Roxanne skeptically. "How about you, Roxanne? What's your topic?"

Roxanne shrugged. "I'm still thinking," she said noncommittally. "To tell the truth, public speaking isn't one of my many talents. I'm not exactly a born speech writer." She cleared her throat. "So you're seeing Vince tomorrow?"

Daniel shot her a questioning look. "Yeah. Something you want me to tell him?"

Daniel knew what had happened at the leadership camp, Roxanne was sure. She colored. "No," she said hastily, hoping that Daniel wouldn't press her any further. What she had to tell Vince couldn't be trusted to anyone else. It was too personal, too important.

"Okay," Daniel said with a shrug. "Vince was going to come to the Market today, but at the last minute he got a call from the rescue squad." He grinned. "You know Vince. He was off like a shot to do his bit to save the world — or his little corner of it, anyway."

A stab of disappointment ran through Roxanne. Vince wasn't coming at all today. She couldn't send him a message directly, but maybe it wouldn't hurt to show Daniel how much she cared. He might even tell Vince, she thought. "Well, I hope he'll come to the fair," she said in a voice that trembled just slightly.

As soon as Daniel left and the two girls were wandering off on their own again, Charlotte said, "You're really upset about not seeing Vince today, aren't you?"

Roxanne nodded. "It's really awful, Char. I wanted to see him so badly. I just have to explain to him — " She stopped. There it was again. She wanted to confide in Charlotte, but she just couldn't. It would be too embarrassing to tell her everything that had gone on, and she couldn't tell part of it without telling the rest.

"Well, you'll see him at the Rotary Club meeting," Charlotte pointed out. "If you decide to go, that is."

"I guess I *have* to go now." Roxanne shivered. "But I'm still scared to death at the idea of getting up and talking in front of all those people. Everybody else's speech will probably be better than mine. I'm afraid I'll look like a fool."

Charlotte put her arm around her friend's shoulders. "No you won't, Rox," she said comfortingly. "Listen, I'll coach you. You just have a simple case of stage fright, that's all. And getting over it isn't really that hard. You'll see."

Roxanne looked at Charlotte gratefully. "Do you really think so?" she asked. "Do you really think you can help me get over being so scared?"

Charlotte nodded. "Sure," she said with a confident smile.

"All right," Roxanne replied, "I'll give it a try." I'll do anything to get Vince back, she thought fiercely, even if I have to make a fool of myself. But with Charlotte's help, maybe she wouldn't *have* to make a fool of herself. Roxanne gave Charlotte another grateful look. What would she do without her friendship?

Chapter
4

"What do you think about this as a lead-in to my speech?" Daniel asked. He picked up his paper and looked over at Vince DiMase, who was sprawled comfortably in a worn, overstuffed chair in the Tacketts' small living room. "How about if I begin by pointing out that *The Red and the Gold* is read by almost two thousand students a week, for approximately thirty-six weeks a year, which means that each weekly column could be read almost seventy-five thousand times during the school year!"

"That's pretty interesting," Vince said, looking up from the clipboard in his lap. He ran his fingers through his thick black hair. "I would never have thought of putting it that way."

"The power of the press," Daniel said proudly. "Never underestimate it, Vince. The press is the key to the opinions of the people and the main-

38

stay of an informed democracy. If *The Red and the Gold* starts picking up some really key issues and explaining them fully, the students are bound to get more interested in what's going on. I mean, football games are fine, but there are more significant problems in the world. It's time that the newspaper took a stand on some of them."

Vince looked surprised. "Don't you think Karen took a stand on some serious stuff last year?" he asked. "I mean, she always covered school board meetings, and remember that editorial she wrote about how teachers ought to be paid more?"

Daniel nodded. Ever since leadership camp, when he and Lin Park had seen how people who really felt strongly could take charge and turn an entire group around, he'd been thinking about the power and the responsibilities of being the paper's editor in chief. "Yeah, sure, Karen did a good job," he admitted. "Compared to most school papers, *The Red and the Gold* is a real standout. But that doesn't mean there isn't a lot of room for improvement. That's what I want to focus on in this speech — quality. There's no reason why *The Red and the Gold* can't be the best newspaper in the state! And if I've got anything to say about it, it *will* be." He pounded emphatically on the arm of the sofa to underline his statement.

Vince blinked at Daniel's intensity. "Your speech sounds pretty revolutionary," he said. "I have the feeling that most Rotary Club members think that the main purpose of the newspaper really is to report the sports news." He looked down at his paper. "I don't think my speech is going to be quite so radical. All I'm going to say is that being at leadership camp really helped me see the importance of being a volunteer. You lead by example. If people helped other people more often, if they tried to see things through other people's eyes, maybe the world would be a little better."

Daniel grinned. Vince was always standing up for the underdog. "Listen, that sounds pretty revolutionary to me," he said. "I'll bet that most people wouldn't even think of getting involved, much less do anything." He got up and stretched. "Want a sandwich? I think there's some liverwurst in the refrigerator."

"Terrific," Vince said, setting down his clipboard. He rubbed his plaid-shirted shoulder ruefully, stretching out a kink. "I get the sense that this kind of thing comes a lot easier to you than it does to me. I'm not exactly a born speech writer. I'd rather *do* things than talk about them."

Daniel led the way into the kitchen of the small tract house he shared with his mother. Opening the refrigerator, he said, "That's just what Roxanne was saying yesterday. About not being a born speech writer, I mean."

Vince sat down on a kitchen stool. "Roxanne?"

"Yeah, I saw her yesterday at the Saturday Market, with Charlotte and the rest of the crowd. Too bad you couldn't come. It was fun." He took out the mayonnaise. "What do you want on your sandwich?"

"Mayo's fine," Vince said, sounding distracted. Then he went on, "Charlotte told me that Roxanne was over her poison ivy."

"Yeah," Daniel said, taking a knife out of a drawer. "It doesn't look like she's gotten over *you*, though. She asked about you, and from the look in her eyes, I'd say she's carrying a torch for you about the size of the one on the Statue of Liberty."

Vince propped his elbows on the counter. "Well, *I've* gotten over her, once and for all. I'm not going to fall for her little tricks ever again."

"You're still mad at her, huh?" Daniel said.

Vince picked up a salt shaker and began to turn it in his fingers. "Well, not exactly. I guess I've gotten over being angry, too. In fact, the farther away I get from that girl, the more I actually feel sorry for her. I mean, take her mother, for example. She obviously couldn't care less about Roxanne. No wonder Roxanne is so insecure. She's so scared that people won't accept her that she tries too hard — that's her problem." He sighed. "I wish I could do something for her, but I can't. It's all over between us, and the sooner she finds somebody else, the better it'll be for her."

Daniel began to slice the liverwurst onto the bread. "I don't think that's quite the way she sees it." In fact, yesterday Roxanne had given him the distinct impression that she was still crazy about Vince.

Vince nodded. "Yeah, I know," he sighed. "I've got to tell her. Maybe it's time to clear the

41

air — now, before school starts and we have to see each other in the halls and out on the quad every day."

Daniel handed Vince his sandwich and got out a bag of potato chips. "So, you're putting women on hold for a while, huh?" It wasn't exactly an idle remark. He'd been a bit disillusioned with them himself after he'd been such an idiot with Lin. If you couldn't make a relationship work with the one girl who really mattered, maybe it would be better not to get involved with girls at all.

"Hey, I didn't say that!" Vince exclaimed with a laugh. He picked up his sandwich and took a bite. "If you want to know the truth, I'm kind of interested in Charlotte DeVries. I got to know her better at leadership camp, and I'm beginning to believe that she's the kind of girl I *thought* Roxanne was — sweet, unselfish, feminine, you know, the sort of old-fashioned girl who puts other people first. The kind that tells you things straight and doesn't try to manipulate you. If you ask me, Charlotte is somebody you can trust."

Daniel raised his eyebrows as he began to eat his own sandwich. Vince might be right, but there was more to Charlotte than old-fashioned southern graciousness and charm. She could be tough and stubborn if she had to be. Maybe Charlotte wasn't the kind who manipulated other people and used them for her own advantage as Roxanne did, but Daniel knew that didn't mean that she wouldn't try to get her own way if she wanted it badly enough.

42

When Vince had finished eating, he glanced at his watch. "It's getting kind of late, and I promised my niece I'd take her and a friend over to the skating rink this afternoon. I guess I'd better be on my way."

Daniel nodded, polishing off the last of his sandwich. "It didn't look like we were going to get a lot more done on our speeches, anyway," he agreed. "Might as well call it quits for now. We can always get back to it later."

After Vince had packed up his things and left, Daniel sat at the kitchen counter, his chin in his hands, thinking. He wished that they hadn't talked about girls. It was a subject he'd been trying very hard not to think about for the last couple of weeks, ever since his disastrous trip to D.C. to see Lin.

But he might as well face up to the truth, Daniel told himself. He hadn't been able to get Lin out of his thoughts ever since he'd first seen her, with her long, dark hair framing her pretty face. But what mattered even more to Daniel, she had a sharp and challenging mind that was continually searching for deeper truths. Her face lingered in his mind, as clear as a photograph, and he could still feel the touch of her slim, delicate fingers on his cheek when he had kissed her. Even though her parents disapproved, even though they expected her to date only Asian boys, there *had* to be a way around them, he thought. There *had* to be a way! Okay, so he'd blown it by going to her house before she'd had a chance to prepare her parents. And maybe he'd really screwed things up when he kissed her in the hallway, right in front of her shocked mother. After that, Lin had told Daniel that it was all over between them. But in spite of what she'd said, he knew that it couldn't be true. He and Lin were made for each other. And no matter what Lin had said, he couldn't just sit around twiddling his thumbs and wishing that the situation could get better. He had to *do* something! But what? What could he do to improve things?

Daniel found himself staring at the telephone on the kitchen wall. What if he called her? It was possible that her parents weren't home, and they could talk undisturbed. If he just had a chance to explain, he was sure that he could make her understand. And even if her parents were home, they couldn't object to a simple telephone call, could they? No matter how strict they were, they couldn't be *that* dictatorial. If one of her parents answered, he'd just be very cool and very polite. They'd *have* to let him speak to her.

Impulsively, Daniel picked up the phone and began to dial the number he already knew by heart. Biting his lip, he waited while it rang once, twice, three times. On the third ring, he heard the receiver being picked up. He took a deep breath.

"Good afternoon," a well-modulated, deeply accented voice said.

Daniel's heart sank. It wasn't Lin, it was her mother. He cleared his throat. "Uh, I'd like to speak to Lin, please."

There was a moment of silence at the other end

of the line. Then the voice spoke in a very polite but chilly tone. "May I tell her who is calling?"

Daniel cleared his throat again. "It's Daniel," he said thickly. "Daniel Tackett."

"I am sorry," the voice said. The chill had turned to ice. "Lin cannot come to the telephone. It would be much better if you did not call again."

Daniel forgot his resolve. "Listen," he said, his tone urgent, "I *have* to talk to her. Please, let me — "

Before he could say another word, there was a loud click. For a long moment, Daniel stared at the receiver in his hand, and then he slammed it down angrily. It wasn't fair! No matter how they felt about him, it wasn't right to refuse to let him talk to her! He couldn't believe this was happening. It was like something out of Romeo and Juliet, where young lovers are separated by the prejudices of their parents.

But this wasn't a play, he reminded himself, closing his eyes and feeling the hurt and disappointment flood through him. It was reality, an unbelievably painful reality. The only way to deal with it was to keep trying to get through, keep trying to make contact. Somehow, he had to bypass Lin's parents and reach her directly. He wasn't sure exactly what he'd do, but he would find a way. He grinned a little, remembering how Lin had disagreed with his idea that if your motives were pure and your goal was worthwhile, that the end would justify almost any means. But he was right, he knew it. Whatever he had to do to see Lin again and talk to her, he would do.

He squared his shoulders, feeling a little bit better now that he had made a decision. He would keep loving Lin, no matter what happened, and he would never give up. And in the meantime, the only way to deal with the situation was to totally immerse himself in working on *The Red and the Gold*.

Chapter
5

Torrey wheeled his bike out of the garage and climbed onto it, smiling a little to himself as he remembered the last time he'd taken it out, just a couple of days ago. He'd been angry and resentful then at having to bike instead of drive. Biking had seemed so dorky. Now, he felt completely different about it. The movie *Breaking Away* had made him see that biking was a real sport. It took lots of strength and endurance — and courage, too. He'd watched the movie a couple of times, and not just with half his mind, the way he usually did things. He'd really *watched* this movie, and before he knew what was happening, he found himself on his bike, taking a long ride out into the country.

For the first time ever, he felt a real sense of freedom and power — pumping up steep hills, coasting down long slopes, feeling the strength in his legs, and the quick, light way the bike responded to his touch. In fact, he felt a lot like the way the main character in *Breaking Away* must have felt when he got on his bike and headed out into the country. The next day he'd done it again, feeling even stronger and better. When he got back home, he'd turned on the VCR and watched the movie one more time.

Now he had to return it. Torrey couldn't help hoping that Sara would be there, although she probably wouldn't talk to him after the crazy way he'd acted — being rude and riding off without thanking her.

Now, as he rode along, he thought about Sara. It was weird how she'd managed to pick *exactly* the right movie for him. In fact, it was more than weird, when you got down to it. A picture of Sara had stayed with him all weekend — her bright eyes, the honey blonde streaks in her hair, her eagerness when she talked about movies. He felt a really strange kind of closeness to her that he couldn't explain. How could she have seen so clearly what he needed? It must have had something to do with fate.

There were two other customers in the Video Stop when Torrey slipped in through the door. Sara had just gotten up from her typewriter to help one of them, so Torrey wandered around the front of the store with the video under his arm, looking at titles on the rack but keeping an eye on Sara. Today she was wearing jeans and a bright yellow shirt, and she looked cheerful and happy as she waited on the first customer and then turned to the second. He could hear her saying something about a movie, talking knowledgeably, with energy and enthusiasm. With a smile, the customer selected the movie she recommended — who wouldn't, he wondered — and left. Sara went back to her typewriter and began to work.

For a few minutes, Torrey stood behind a big revolving rack, trying to decide what to do. He had been pretty rude the other day. Maybe it would be better to just put the video into the box by the front door and duck out. Or maybe. . . .

At that moment, Sara looked up from her typewriter, and Torrey could tell she'd seen him. She stood up and hesitated for an instant. Then she came toward him. There was an uncertain smile on her face.

"Hi," she said. She cleared her throat. "I, uh, I hope you liked the movie." When Torrey didn't say anything, she went on, stumbling a little over her words. "I mean, um, I usually don't make a practice of forcing movies on people the way I did with you. I hope you, uh, don't think I was just trying to make a sale or something. Business is slow sometimes, but it isn't *that* slow."

Torrey relaxed, and then he grinned. So she wasn't mad at him after all, the way most girls would have been. In fact, most girls would have tried to make him feel like a jerk for the way he'd acted. "Hey, it's okay," he said. "I really *liked* the movie."

Sara's smile broadened. "Really?" she asked, and Torrey could hear the relief in her voice. "I mean, you're not just telling me that to make me feel better, are you?"

"No, really," Torrey assured her. "In fact, I actually went out for a couple of long rides, which is a miracle for me. Four-wheel-drive and an open road's more my style. Anyway, biking was . . . pretty okay. . . . " He stopped. She didn't want to hear that stuff. He held out the videocassette and said, "Here, I hope I haven't worn it out. I, uh, watched it a couple of times." He stared at his feet. "And I guess I owe you an apology, too," he said. "For being such a jerk when you were trying to help me."

Sara took the cassette. Looking down, she said, "I'm glad you liked it." She turned to go back to the counter. "I'll check it in for you."

Torrey followed her. In spite of his nervousness, he didn't want this conversation to end. He cleared his throat, watching Sara pull a yellow ticket out of a file and scribble something on it. "Um, you were really on the mark with this movie, and . . . well, maybe you could recommend some others to me."

Sara put the video back on the shelf behind her. "Sure," she said, turning around with a smile. "I'd be glad to. What kind of movies do you like — besides biking movies, that is?"

Torrey shrugged, feeling uncomfortable under Sara's inquiring gaze. "I don't know," he muttered. "I mean, movies are usually just something to fill up the time with."

Sara laughed. "A lot of them are like that," she

admitted. "After you've seen them, you don't really know what you've seen. But there are some that really make an impression on you. It's like they're really about *your* life. Do you know what I mean?"

Torrey nodded. "Yeah," he answered slowly. He leaned both elbows on the counter, thinking about it. "*Breaking Away* was like that. I mean, it showed me that you really *can* break away from the bad stuff in your life if you really — "

He stopped, flushing. What *was* it about this girl that made him blabber so much? Why couldn't he act cool around her? Next thing he knew, he'd be telling her his life story. No matter how nice she seemed or how willing to listen, he wasn't about to let his defenses down. And anyway, if he did, she'd probably stop being nice in an instant.

But Sara didn't seem to be making any judgments. "I like those kinds of movies, too," she said. She took a tape off the shelf. "Like this one, for instance. It's about a girl who's really determined to be a dancer. She'll do anything to get a chance to dance, even give up her boyfriend, if she has to. But she figures out after a while that it's better if she doesn't focus her life so narrowly on dancing, that there's got to be love, too. In the end she gets both."

Torrey laughed shortly, suddenly hating the happy picture Sara had painted in his mind. "The old happy ending, huh? Well, out in the real world, things aren't like that. In real life, you have to give up one thing to get something else, and sometimes you wind up losing on *both* counts."

Sara gazed up at him with a curious look. "That's a pretty cynical view of the world, isn't it?"

"Maybe," Torrey replied defensively. "But you have to take the world the way it is, not the way you want it to be. It's better to be cynical about things than to expect too much. That way you won't be disappointed when things don't turn out the way you want." His grin was bleak. "Believe me, I know."

Sara's blue eyes became troubled, and she turned back to the shelf. "Well, here's another movie that I think is really good," she said with forced brightness. She handed him the video of *Pretty in Pink*. "Molly Ringwald is in it, and she's really good. The character I like most, though, is her father. I guess he reminds me of my dad — sort of flaky and crazy, a real softie at heart. I live with my dad."

"Yeah?" Torrey raised his eyebrows. "Your folks divorced?"

Sara nodded. "It's just been Dad and me for the last couple of years, all by ourselves."

That made something else they had in common, Torrey thought. "My parents are divorced, too," he said. "I live with my mother. And my sister," he added, as an afterthought. "My sister's a total drag most of the time. And I *hate* living with Mom."

Sara seemed surprised. "Really? Why?"

"Why? A million reasons. She only thinks of herself," he said bitterly. "She never thinks about me or Rox, we never do anything together — we don't even eat together. All that freedom sounds great, right? Everyone says I should just be glad she lets me do what I want. But it's like she doesn't even care. Like we're some kind of awful inconvenience or something. And now she's involved with this guy who acts like he's my father and tries to order me around."

"Where's your real father?"

"He lives in D.C.," Torrey said. He paused, thinking about it. "You know, it would be okay if my real father wanted to tell me what to do, but he's just like dear old Mom." He sighed. "All he ever does is buy me presents and stuff, like the bike and my stereo, as if that'll make up for everything. I asked if I could go live with him last year, to get away from Mom and Roxanne, but he said no. He said he was too involved in his business, and he didn't have time for a kid."

"That's too bad," Sara said. Torrey looked at her. In her blue eyes he saw a sad look of sympathy. It was strange to tell somebody how he felt, Torrey thought, and even stranger to have them understand. "It's too bad when parents can't be really close to their children," she added slowly. "I'm glad that my dad is different."

"Different how?" Torrey asked.

Sara shook her head, looking down. "You don't really want to know, do you? I mean, if you're just trying to be polite. . . ."

"No, I really want to know," Torrey told her.

It was true. He really *did* want to hear what her father was like, why he was different. "I was beginning to get the idea that all fathers were sort of alike," he added. "Most of my friends' fathers don't pay much attention to them, either."

"Well, my father's not like that at all," Sara said quickly. She looked down at the video in her hands. "He's . . . well, he's home a lot of the time, for one thing."

"Doesn't he work?" Torrey thought of his father, who worked all the time and was so busy that he had to send his secretary out to buy Christmas presents.

Sara laughed a little. "Sure, he works. Well, sometimes, anyway. I told you, he's sort of like Molly Ringwald's father in the movie. He works enough for us to get by on. Actually, it's kind of hard for him to keep a job." Torrey wanted to ask why, but he decided he'd better not. Sara went on in a kind of dreamy voice. "But it's really okay — that he doesn't work regularly, I mean. It gives us time to be together. That's the best part of having a father, being *with* him. Having him there when I come home, always ready to talk, to help me get over the bad spots."

Torrey looked at her, feeling a little prickle of envy. "Yeah," he said, "that sure would be nice."

"Actually, he's my best friend," Sara added. She looked up at Torrey. Her eyes were so blue and clear that he felt he could have stared into them forever. But then she turned away, as if she was hiding something. But what? "We do a lot of things together," she was saying. "We go fish-

54

ing in Chesapeake Bay and to the museums in D.C. and to the movies." She laughed a little. "And sometimes we just hang around the living room and eat popcorn and watch old movies on TV. You know, just to relax. Those are the best times of all. Just hanging out together."

In the front of the store, the bell on the door tinkled as a customer came in and began to browse through the video racks. Torrey straightened up. "I think I'll take this one," he said, indicating *Pretty in Pink*. "Maybe it'll give me an idea of what your dad is like."

Sara colored a little. "Maybe," she said. She began to write up the ticket. "Do you want to put this on your mom's charge?" Her voice was businesslike.

Torrey reached for his wallet. "No, I'll pay for it," he said. When the customer came in, he'd suddenly started feeling stiff and formal. But inside, he still felt warm . . . and strange. Torrey had never really been close to anyone before. Sure, there were kids around school and at the Hall of Fame he hung out with, but he didn't really know anything about them and vice versa. But here was someone who actually seemed to care about him. It was weird, but he wanted to find out more about her, to learn what she was really like. And he couldn't just keep dropping into the Video Stop, hoping to meet her, trying to catch her when she wasn't busy. Maybe he should ask her out.

"Listen, uh, Sara," he said quickly, before he lost his nerve, "how would you like to — " Sud-

55

denly he stopped. What an idiot he was. He couldn't ask her out. He didn't have any wheels — unless you counted his bike, that is.

"What?" Sara asked. She leaned forward, her blue eyes holding his. "What were you going to say?"

"I — I was going to ask," Torrey began hesitantly, "if you'd go out with me. But then I remembered that I don't have a car right now." He paused and added in a bitter tone, "My sister and I got into a fight over the car, and then George, my mom's boyfriend, told me I couldn't drive for the next two months. So I guess that means I can't ask you for a real date. All I've got is my bike, and it's not the kind of bike that you can ride somebody on."

Sara thought about this for a moment. "Well, a car doesn't matter so much. Anyway, I've got to work here almost every night this week. But I have an idea — next Saturday, the Rotary Club is sponsoring a presentation at the Holiday Inn over on Pershing Avenue. My dad thought it would be a good idea for me to go. Maybe you'd like to go, too. We could sit together, maybe talk for a little while afterward, if you want."

"A presentation?" Torrey said doubtfully. "What kind of presentation?"

"Have you heard about the leadership camp they hold every year? A few kids from each school in the D.C. area go there to learn how to better run student activities — "

"Yeah," Torrey cut in sharply. "My sister went this year."

"She did?" Sara said, raising her eyebrows. She looked impressed. "Well, the kids who went are going to give talks about their experiences. One of the guys is the new editor of *The Red and the Gold*, Daniel Tackett."

Torrey nodded. "Yeah, I know Daniel. He was the editor of the paper at Stevenson High, where I used to go."

Sara's face held a look of barely suppressed excitement. "Well, this fall I'm going to try to sell Daniel on the idea that *The Red and the Gold* ought to have its very own film critic — *me*."

Torrey cocked his head, looking at her. The more he found out about this girl, the more he liked her. "You know, Sara, that's a pretty good idea. Everyone goes to the movies."

"That's what Dad thought, too," Sara said. "In fact, it was Dad's idea to go hear what Daniel has to say about his plans for the paper. Then, when I talk to Daniel about the film column, I can make sure my idea fits in with his overall plans."

Torrey sighed. "Well, we still haven't solved the problem of transportation."

"Oh, that's okay," Sara said breezily. "Dad's offered to drive me to hear the presentations and pick me up afterward. He's really supportive. He'll do *anything* to help me achieve my goals — even if he has to give up something important that *he* wants to do." She smiled at him. "So what do you think? Would you like to come?"

Torrey cringed inside at the thought of sitting through Roxanne's speech. She'd probably brag and show off, just the way she did at home. And what if any of his friends found out he went? It was such a *responsible* thing to do — they'd never let him live it down. But Sara's sweet smile and the inviting look in her blue eyes overwhelmed him.

"Okay," he said, picking up the video and tucking it under his arm. "I'll be there."

"Oh, that's *great*, Torrey," Sara exclaimed happily. "Now I'll *really* look forward to going to hear the speeches!"

Chapter
6

"Well, one good thing about it being so cold out today is that the beach isn't crowded," Jonathan told Lily as they spread their beach blanket over the sand. "We've got it all to ourselves. Well, almost," he added, as a couple of jeeps roared along the sand road behind them, the drivers shouting to one another.

Lily shivered and zipped up her red sweatshirt against the cool breeze. She was glad she'd worn it, along with her sweatpants, over her swimsuit. Fall *was* definitely on its way. Even the seagulls skimming the gray waves looked chilly. "I think I'd rather have the sun," she said, "even if it does mean lots of people. I hope it warms up before the fair next week."

"Yeah, me, too," Jonathan said. He flopped down on the blanket with a huge, dejected sigh and tilted his fedora forward over his eyes. "I can't believe it's the end of August already."

Lily sat down beside Jonathan and ran her fingers through her short, wavy blonde hair. "Yeah, Brian and Karen left for Brown yesterday; I ran into Karen at the mall before she left. She was really excited about all her new clothes and the stuff she's been getting for her dorm room." Lily smiled a little. "I'll bet she's going to be so busy with all her new friends that she won't have time to think about us. I doubt she'll even have time to miss *The Red and the Gold*."

His eyes still shut, Jonathan reached out for Lily's hand. "Well, I don't know about missing *The Red and the Gold* after I get to Penn, but you can bet I'll miss everyone." He sighed again. "I'm so nervous, so scared of leaving. And the funny thing is, I'm not even sure exactly why. It's almost as bad as it was this spring."

Lily squeezed Jonathan's hand and then let it go as she reached for her beach bag. Even if the sun was hidden under a cloud, she knew she'd better put some sunscreen on her nose.

Jonathan opened his eyes and frowned at her. His usually easygoing face was taut and strained, and he looked hurt. "Sorry," he said briefly. "I guess I've been boring you with all my problems lately."

Lily sighed. Jonathan had been on edge again for the past month, and his feelings had been extrasensitive, easily wounded. Obviously, the strain of leaving Rose Hill and going away to college was getting to him in a big way, making him tense and anxious. And the more tension and anxiety he felt, the more sensitive he became. Even though they still managed to have a good time when they were together, it was taking a lot of patience these days to cope with his moods. And patience wasn't always Lily's strong point.

She reached out and squeezed his hand again before she opened the plastic bottle of sunscreen. "I'm not bored, Jonathan," she said, managing a smile. "And I *do* know how you feel, honestly. I feel that way, too, sometimes, before I go on-stage. I get this knotted-up feeling in my stomach, and I'm scared and jittery. Sometimes I even feel like I'm going to faint." She began to dab the sunscreen on her nose.

"Yeah?" Jonathan relaxed a little, sounding interested. "Tell me more, doc. You got a cure for this awful disease? Do people die from it?"

Lily laughed. This was more like the old Jonathan. "No, people don't die from it, silly. It's called stage fright. Almost all performers suffer from it at least once in their careers." She pulled her sunglasses down to the tip of her nose and peered at him over the rims. "My expert diagnosis, sir," she said in a pompous, doctorish voice, "is that you're suffering from a special and extremely virulent strain of the disease that seems to afflict certain people during the month of August. It's called college fright." She giggled and pushed her glasses back up on her nose.

Jonathan looked at her seriously. "Yeah, well, maybe that's what it is. I have to admit that I'm worried about all kinds of stuff — roommates, classes. I won't know where I'm going, and I'll have to carry around a map like a stupid freshman. What if there's hazing? What if the food's as lousy as Kennedy's? And besides, Penn is a *big* school — it's going to take me forever to make the kind of friends I've got here." He shut his eyes briefly, adding in a wistful tone, "There'll never be another bunch of kids like this crowd."

Lily nodded. "I know," she said reflectively, watching a small bird darting into the waves. "It *will* be different, with so many kids leaving." She smiled to herself. "That's not bad, because things *always* change. Nothing ever stays the same. In fact, it'll really be fun to see how everyone changes, after the seniors are gone."

She stopped guiltily, glancing at Jonathan. That hadn't been a very smart thing to say, given the way he was feeling. He was part of the old group, and it wasn't a good idea to remind him that life at Kennedy would go on in the same interesting, exciting way without him and the others. She got to her feet. "Hey, how about if I go up to the snack bar and get us both something to drink?"

Jonathan started to get up. "I'll go with you," he said quickly.

"No, that's okay," Lily said, feeling closed in again. Couldn't she even go to the snack bar by herself? "I'll be back in a minute."

Jonathan shrugged. "Well, if you insist," he said. "But don't be long. Okay?"

Lily trudged slowly up the beach, kicking at

the sand. Why were things so tense and uneasy? She would have thought that with Jonathan going away, they'd be savoring every last, loving minute together — the way other couples were. Lily sighed. It wasn't exactly easy to have to deal with Jonathan's moods and cope with his possessiveness. She still cared for him — when he forgot about his problems, he was still the same wild, crazy Jonathan he'd always been — but it was getting harder and harder to care the way she used to. In fact, to tell the truth, there was a little part of Lily that was actually looking forward to next week, after Jonathan was gone. She folded her arms tightly across her chest. It was hard not to feel guilty about that.

At the snack bar, she ordered two Cokes, trading friendly hellos with the cute guy at the cash register, then carried the cups back down the beach. She sat down close to Jonathan and handed him one.

"So," she said brightly, "what are you going to do with Big Pink while you're gone?" Big Pink was Jonathan's beloved '57 Chevy.

Jonathan sat up and put his arm around her, laughing a little. "Big Pink's got a special place reserved in the garage," he said. "My folks say I can leave her there so I can use her when I'm home on vacation." His arm tightened. "That way, we can go to all the old places, just like always."

"Great," Lily said absently. She noticed two boys jogging down the beach toward them, running with long, loping strides. As they got closer, she recognized them. They were both members of the Kennedy High Drama Club. At the same moment, they recognized her and altered their course to jog up the beach in her direction.

"Hi, Lily," the first one called, flashing her a broad smile. "How's your summer going?"

"It's been great," Lily said. The boys stopped beside the blanket to talk. "Way too short, as usual. I can't believe it's almost time for school to start again." She half-turned toward Jonathan. "You guys know Jonathan Preston, don't you? He'll be leaving for Penn next week. Jonathan, this is Pete Mitchell and Larry Hinson, from the Drama Club at Kennedy."

"Penn, huh?" Larry said. He pulled one foot up behind him, doing a jogger's thigh stretch. "My cousin went there. He really liked it. He says Penn's got a super drama program."

"Oh, yeah?" Jonathan said briefly. "That's good, if you're into drama."

Larry turned his attention to Lily. "Hey, did you hear about the new drama teacher?"

Lily sat up straighter, "A new teacher? Who?"

"Her name is Mrs. Weiss," Pete chimed in. "Larry and I met her last week when we went over to school to pick up my sister after cheerleading tryouts. She's been teaching in D.C., and she says she's got some really hot plans for our club." He grinned. "I liked her a lot. She's young and she's got a lot of personality. You know, one of those really gung-ho types."

"Plans?" Lily asked eagerly. "What kind of plans?"

"She says we're going to be the best Drama Club in the state," Larry said. "With her help, of course."

"And she's going to start us off with Shakespeare's *Twelfth Night* — a shortened version of it, anyway." Pete said. "Sounds like it's going to be a really interesting production, with lots of special effects. Tryouts will be the second week of September, she said." He began to jog in place, his eyes bright with excitement. "If we start with something as challenging as Shakespeare, just think where we'll be by the end of the year!"

Lily felt a sudden rush of excitement. "Wow, what a great opportunity," she said softly, trying to imagine what it would be like to have a role in *Twelfth Night* — maybe even the female lead. She had always loved the lilt and poetry of Shakespeare's language, even if it wasn't always so easy to understand.

"Yeah," Larry said. "I know what you mean. I've always liked Kennedy's drama program, but I've had the feeling that we were kind of stuck in a rut, doing the same sort of thing all the time. It was great to meet Mrs. Weiss and hear about all the changes she's planning."

Lily turned to Jonathan. "Isn't it great?" she asked. "A new coach can make an incredible difference."

"Yeah," Jonathan said. "Yeah, great. It's really great." His voice was quiet, with a sarcastic undertone. All he could think of was his ex-girlfriend Fiona, and how her involvement with Kennedy's production of *Oklahoma!* had threatened to break them up forever. "I'm sure you'll have a really terrific time."

Lily stared at him. He sounded as if he *resented* the fact that she was going to be involved and doing things, that she wouldn't be sitting at home all by herself pining for him.

Larry threw an uncomfortable glance at Jonathan and turned to Pete. "We'd better be on our way if we're going to get back in time for lunch."

Pete nodded and grinned. "Good to meet you, Jonathan. Hope you have a good year at Penn." He looked at Lily. "And I'll see you when school starts. Are you going to try out for *Twelfth Night*?"

"Absolutely," Lily vowed. "I'll see you at the tryouts."

After the guys left, Lily was silent for a moment. She picked up a handful of sand, sifting the grains through her fingers, feeling them slip away. Jonathan didn't say anything either. He was sitting up, staring bleakly out at the gray water, watching a lone gull fishing in the waves. Finally he said, "I'm sorry." He still didn't look at her.

Lily picked up another handful of sand and let it run out of her fingers. "What made you act like that?" she asked.

Jonathan shrugged. "I don't know," he said sullenly. Then he turned to her, his eyes dark.

66

"Yeah, I do," he said. "I'm acting this way because I'm scared."

"Scared of going away, you mean?"

Jonathan shook his head. "No, it's not that so much as. . . . " His voice drifted off. "I mean, yeah, sure, I'm nervous about going to Penn. After all, I've spent my whole life here in Rose Hill, and leaving is rough. But it's more than that. It's you."

Lily stared at him. "*Me*?"

"Yeah, you." Jonathan reached for her hand. "I could see the way those guys looked at you. You're so pretty, and you've got such a great personality, so much enthusiasm and dedication to being an actress. I'm afraid that after I'm gone nothing will ever be the same between us. I'm afraid I'll lose you. You'll get so busy with the Drama Club and that crowd and — " He stopped and cleared his throat. "I have the feeling that you'll forget all about me."

Lily wasn't sure how to respond. She hesitated, and then she said, very carefully, "That's just not true, Jonathan, and you know it. Or at least you ought to. We've been so close, I could never forget what we've had together, or what we've been to one another."

Jonathan stared at her, still holding on to her hand. His jaw muscles tightened, and there was a red flush high on each cheek. "You're making it sound like it's already over. Like you've already written us off."

Lily laughed a little, as lightly as she could.

"Well, part of it is over, isn't it? I mean, this part of our relationship can't go on forever. I haven't written us off, but we can't pretend that things aren't going to change for us. *You're* changing, aren't you? You'll be away at Penn, in a new place, with new friends and maybe even a new — "

Jonathan interrupted her, his voice rough and edged with tension. "A new place, yes. New friends, probably. But not a new *girlfriend*. You're the only girlfriend I want, Lily. You're the one I *need*. I'll never stop feeling that way about you, and I don't want you to stop feeling that way about me." His fingers tightened around her hand, and his voice took on a different tone. "I want us to go on feeling the same way about each other that we feel right now . . . forever. I can't stand the thought of losing you."

Lily looked at him. Was that *panic* she was hearing in his voice? He was holding her hand so tightly that it hurt. What could she say to him that would help him stop being afraid?

"I don't want to lose you, either, Jonathan," she said at last. "I want us to go on feeling the way we do now." She leaned toward him. "I need you, too."

"Really?" Jonathan asked. Some of the fear went out of his eyes. "Are you telling me the truth?"

Lily nodded. "The truth, the whole truth, and nothing but the truth," she said, and laughed a little.

"Then we don't have anything to worry about," Jonathan said. He looked at her intently. "Do we?"

"No," Lily said. "We don't." And she leaned forward to kiss him.

Chapter
7

Roxanne loved the way Charlotte had fixed up her bedroom. In fact, she loved Charlotte's entire house — an elegant, two-story mansion in the expensive hillside neighborhood behind Kennedy High. But although the entire house was impressive, with its southern-style architecture and its luxurious decor, Charlotte's bedroom was something extraspecial. The walls were painted a delicate shade of rose, and the drapes and the velvety carpet were a pale blue. The queen-size bed had a ruffled pink canopy, and it was covered with a fluffy pink satin quilt. The delicate furniture was painted an antique ivory, softly edged in gilt, and the mirror over Charlotte's dressing table was gold-framed, too. Over in the corner, an antique music stand was used to display a rainbow of pretty ribbons, and the hat Charlotte had bought at the Saturday Market hung on the corner. Charlotte's soft floral perfume filled the air. Compared to her own bedroom — which was decorated in no particular style at all — Charlotte's room looked like something out of the movies — so cozy and inviting.

This afternoon, Roxanne had come over to practice her speech with Charlotte and get the coaching her friend had promised. The night before, she had spent nearly three hours writing the speech, which was on the importance of leadership training for every student. Charlotte, dressed in a slim, stylish, white cotton jumpsuit, was sitting cross-legged on the pink satin quilt, listening while Roxanne stood in the middle of the room self-consciously reading what she'd written from the cards she held in her hand.

" 'And in conclusion,' " Roxanne said stiffly, " 'I want to thank you for offering me the opportunity to attend leadership camp. It was an experience that I will remember all my life. I know that other students will benefit from the camp, too.' "

In the middle of the bed, Charlotte lifted a polite hand to her mouth to cover a small yawn.

"That bad, huh?" Roxanne asked, sitting down on the foot of the bed. She sighed and kicked off her tennis shoes. "Listen, Charlotte, maybe I should just cancel out of this thing. I can always say I've come down with a bad case of laryngitis and I can't talk. If I get up there and make an idiot out of myself, I'm not going to impress

Vince anyway. And that's who I'm doing this for. I don't give two hoots about the stupid Rotary Club."

"It shows, too." Charlotte tossed her blonde hair and then stared levelly at Roxanne. "I was just kidding, really. Your speech isn't *bad* exactly — in fact, the idea is pretty good, and I like the way you've organized it. The main problem is that it's a little slow in spots. You need to work on your delivery. You know, spice it up a little."

"My delivery?" Roxanne asked, looking doubtful.

"You know, the way you present your speech. You've got some really super ideas — like when you say that our schools ought to teach kids leadership the same way they teach them English and math. But you don't *emphasize* your main points, so everything just sort of blurs together, and it's hard to tell what's important and what isn't. Here, let me show you what I mean."

With that, Charlotte jumped off the bed and took Roxanne's notes, shuffling them quickly until she found what she wanted. Then she pulled the ribbons and the hat off the music stand and set the stand in the middle of the floor to hold Roxanne's notes.

" 'Ladies and gentlemen,' " she read, speaking in a firm, clear voice from her place behind the music stand, " 'I would like to speak to you today about training leaders.' " She caught Roxanne's gaze and held it for a moment. " 'I believe that our schools ought to *teach* leadership.' " She paused dramatically, still watching Roxanne.

72

" 'After all, they teach students how to write and how to solve mathematical equations — two important skills. Why then shouldn't they teach students how to be *leaders*?' " She paused again and leaned forward. " 'We can't just wait for people to *catch* leadership the way they accidentally catch measles or mumps. The only sure way to get good leaders is to *train* them. Don't you agree?' " She stopped and looked at Roxanne. "See the difference?"

Roxanne nodded enviously. Charlotte really knew how to capture an audience. Even though she, Roxanne, had written those lines, she hardly recognized them after the way Charlotte had delivered them.

"Sure, I see the difference," she said. "But I could never do what you're doing. It's . . . it's like *acting*! And you changed some stuff — you turned one of my statements into a question. It's as if you were talking directly *to* the audience, almost like you expect them to answer."

"Exactly!" Charlotte exclaimed. "You ask questions because you want your audience to get involved, to start thinking. You want them to come up with the same answer you came up with. And when you deliver a speech, you are acting, just the way you would be if you were an actress in a play."

"Oh, so now I've got to be an actress, too," Roxanne said with a little laugh. "Maybe that's why I get stage fright every time I think about getting up in front of all those people." Roxanne wondered how Charlotte could manage to be so self-confident, when *she* wanted to sink through the floor at just the *thought* of talking to such a large crowd.

Charlotte smiled sympathetically. "Stage fright is easy to get over, Rox," she said. "All you have to do is to pretend to yourself that everybody in the audience is stark naked."

Roxanne stared at her friend and laughed. Stark naked? What was Charlotte talking about? How could that possibly help — except maybe to distract her?

"Don't you see?" Charlotte asked her, still smiling. "It works every time. If you imagine that your audience isn't wearing any clothes, you'll see there's nothing to be afraid of. They're all just people, like you and me." She held out her hand. "Come here. I want to show you another trick you can use when you're delivering your speech."

Roxanne stood up. "What?"

Charlotte pointed to the music stand. "Chances are good that you'll be standing behind a podium with a microphone on it. That'll give you someplace to put your notes so you won't have to hold them. We can use this music stand for now. And if you don't have your hands full of notes, you'll be able to move them. Here, do what I do." She went through the same passage again, gesturing with her hands to underscore the emphasis in her voice, while Roxanne followed her lead, feeling stiff and awkward.

"Now," Charlotte said when they'd run through it once, "you start at the beginning again and let me be the audience." She sat down on the bed. "Remember, you're an actress. Use your voice *and* your hands to help you make your points. And don't keep looking at your notes all the time. You have to know your speech so well that you're able to make eye contact with your audience. That helps to keep their attention, too."

Feeling a little silly, Roxanne repeated the first couple of paragraphs of her speech, trying her best to imitate Charlotte's graceful motions.

"Stop a second," Charlotte said, interrupting her. "Don't move. Look at yourself in the mirror."

Puzzled, Roxanne glanced at herself. Her hair was tousled, and her red-print blouse was coming untucked. "My hair needs brushing, if that's what you mean." she said. "And my blouse needs straightening."

Charlotte grinned. "No, silly, not your hair. Look at your *posture*."

Roxanne looked again. One hip was out of line because she was putting all of her weight on the other foot. It was a slouch she'd cultivated a year or so ago because she'd thought it was sexy. But now she had gotten into the habit of standing that way.

Charlotte nodded. "Try to imagine that you have a string fastened to the very top of your head and that somebody's pulling up on it, keeping it taut. If you can picture that string in your mind, you won't have any trouble keeping your shoulders relaxed and your spine straight. In fact, you'll practically float. See, like this." She stood up and demonstrated with a few graceful steps and a pirouette.

As Roxanne watched her friend, she felt a slight twinge of frustration. It was clear that Charlotte knew exactly what she was talking about. She moved with a light, easy grace that *did* almost make her seem to float across the room, like a dancer. And now that she thought about it, she remembered admiring Charlotte's graceful walk the very first time they'd met.

"What I want to know, Charlotte," she said, feeling the envy growing inside her, "is where you learned all this stuff. Not just about how to walk, but about how to use your voice and your hands and your eyes, that kind of thing. Did you just figure it out all by yourself?"

Charlotte laughed a little, almost as if she were embarrassed by the question. "Oh, no, not at all! When I was ten or eleven and we were living back in Alabama, my mother thought it would be a good idea if I went to charm school, the way she did when she was young. You know, to learn the right social graces so I could be a credit to my family. All my friends went, too. It was sort of the 'in' thing to do — and kind of fun, actually."

"You mean, you learned all that before you were twelve?" Roxanne asked in disbelief.

"Well, not exactly. Actually, I learned a lot of it from the coaches in the Miss Teen USA Pageant a couple of years ago. We had to give a speech for the competition, as well as make a talent presentation, and they coached us until we thought we'd drop."

As Charlotte told her this, Roxanne's mouth fell open. She couldn't believe it. "You were in a beauty contest?" she asked breathlessly. "How did you do? I mean, did you win?" What a wonderful shock, finding out that her *best* friend was a beauty queen. Wait until the crowd found out about this!

Charlotte nodded. "I won in the local competitions," she said reminiscently. "I even got as far as the state finals, but my grandmother died on the day before the pageant. We all agreed that it would be a good idea for me to drop out, so I did."

Roxanne let out her breath in an explosive sigh. "Oh, Char, what an awful thing to happen!"

"Yes, it was. I was too upset about my grandmother to really think about the contest, but later I realized that I'd had a lot of valuable coaching and had met some wonderful girls. . . . I still write to some of them." She shrugged. "Anyway, even if I'd stayed in, I might not have won."

"Sure, but you *might* have," Roxanne said wistfully. "And if you'd won, you would have gone on to the nationals. Why, Char," she added, awestruck at the thought, "you might have been Miss Teen USA! Don't you ever think about the exciting life you might have led if you'd won? Don't you ever get a little resentful for losing an opportunity like that?"

Charlotte smiled and shrugged. "Well, I suppose I think about it sometimes. But how could I really be angry? Anyway, there's no point brooding over things that are in the past, things you can't change. When something like that happens, the best thing to do is put it behind you."

77

"I know all that," Roxanne said impatiently, "but still, winning the Miss Teen USA pageant would have been — "

"But now," Charlotte interrupted, "I'm too busy with all the exciting things in my life to begin worrying about it. I mean, I'm happy to be in Rose Hill and to have such special friends. It's really terrific to think about all the great times we're going to have in our senior year. Being student activities director is going to be so much fun!"

There was a soft knock at the door, and Charlotte's mother opened it. "I just wanted to remind you, honey," she said, with a gracious smile for Roxanne, "we promised your father we'd pick him up after work so that we can all go out to dinner together. We have to leave in about twenty minutes."

"Oh, that's right," Charlotte said guiltily. Her mother closed the door again, and Charlotte turned to Roxanne. "Let's go over your speech once more before I have to leave, so we can see what you need to work on this week."

Roxanne went to the middle of the room and stood behind the music stand where she could keep an eye on her notes. Trying to remember all the useful things Char had told her, she went through her speech one more time. It went much better this time, and Roxanne felt much more at ease, much less self-conscious.

"Bravo!" Charlotte cried happily, clapping her hands. "That was really good, Rox! Now, all you have to do is go over it a few more times until you know it almost by heart. Then you won't have any trouble making eye contact with your audience."

"It feels a lot better already, Char," Roxanne said. She touched Charlotte's arm. "You know," she said, dropping her eyes almost shyly, "I've never had a friend like you before. I mean, somebody I feel I can really look up to and respect." Not even Frankie was that way. She'd been a good friend — a better friend than Rox realized at the time — but she was . . . well, she'd been a follower, not an equal, someone Roxanne could often manipulate. It had seemed as if Rox always had to lead the way. With Charlotte, things were different. Rox blushed a little. "I just mean that you're special," she said embarrassed. "You're so talented and gifted, but so generous and open, too."

Obviously touched, Charlotte gave Roxanne a warm hug. "I really value our friendship, too, Rox. It means a lot to me to have a friend I can really talk to, really share things with. And we're both lucky to have such a warm loyal group of friends."

Roxanne could only nod. It was true, at least as far as Charlotte was concerned. The crowd had accepted her from the very beginning, recognizing her for the generous, loving person she was. And Roxanne was grateful that Charlotte had singled her out to be her closest friend!

Chapter
8

The Lincoln Room at the Rose Hill Holiday Inn was almost completely filled with members of the Rotary Club. Charlotte noticed that there were a few students there, too. A couple of photographers were even there from the local newspapers, their cameras clicking away at the back of the room. Charlotte was sitting in the front row with the other speakers, wearing a silky, violet-print dress with a swishy skirt — one of her favorites. She had spoken first, and she'd done so with smoothness and confidence. Given some of the audiences she'd performed for, the Rose Hill Rotary Club was a cinch — even if there *were* a few unexpected reporters!

Still, she'd been pleased by the burst of applause at the end, applause she knew she had earned, not just because of what she'd said but because of the *way* she'd said it. She knew she'd done a good job giving her talk, and now she could relax and enjoy the other presentations.

Next to her, Roxanne squirmed uncomfortably, and Charlotte gave her hand a quick, reassuring squeeze. Roxanne was so tense and nervous you'd think she was running for president, Charlotte thought. She smiled a little to herself as Vince DiMase finished his speech about his volunteer work with the Rose Hill Volunteer Rescue Squad, and the audience applauded. Vince was probably the reason for a big part of Roxanne's nervousness. Dressed in a jacket and tie, he really did look gorgeous, and Roxanne was drinking in the sight with hungry eyes.

Actually, Charlotte could understand why her friend had such a crush on Vince. With his broad shoulders and square-jawed face, he was very good-looking in a rugged, he-man way. And he had such a gentlemanly personality, too. He was so straightforward and unpretentious and natural. You could tell by looking at him that Vince was the kind you could always depend on to do the right thing and to tell the truth. It was a quality that Charlotte admired very much. In fact, if she were honest with herself, she would have to admit that it would be very easy to like Vince — a lot. But of course, liking Vince was out of the question because of her friendship with Roxanne. Although she liked to flirt — harmlessly, of course — Charlotte had always practiced a very strict code of ethics, and boyfriend-snatching was certainly not on the list of things she permitted herself to do.

Now it was Roxanne's turn to give her speech. Charlotte watched her friend as she walked to the podium, raised her eyes, and began to speak. In her sophisticated green dress, Roxanne looked especially striking. She really did have movie-star looks. And the extra effort that Charlotte had put into coaching her had paid off, too. Roxanne spoke easily, using just the right gestures and emphasis, almost never looking down at her notes. And she was standing straight and tall, holding herself gracefully instead of poking one hip out, the way she usually did.

Charlotte smiled again. Really, with just a little coaching and encouragement, Roxanne could be a real leader at Kennedy. In fact, it was a shame that no one had recognized her leadership abilities before this and made sure that she'd been given an important position at school for the coming year.

For a minute, it crossed Charlotte's mind to wonder why people hadn't picked up on Roxanne's real potential. There were those rumors about Roxanne fixing up computer dates with several boys at the Valentine's Day Dance, and there was that silly old gossip about the bad blood between the Stevenson transfer students and the Kennedy crowd, but surely that was all water under the bridge now. It was time the crowd recognized Roxanne's real talents and rewarded them. And *she* could help by continuing to encourage Roxanne to make the most of herself. Of course, it wouldn't be easy for Roxanne to change. Her mother wasn't exactly the most car-ing person in the world, and some of the kids thought that her brother, no matter how good-looking he was, was nothing but a punk. But even with the lack of support at home, Roxanne had the potential to go far at Kennedy High. And Charlotte loved the idea of helping her friend realize that potential — and making sure that others saw it, too.

Roxanne finished her speech with a flourish, and the audience began to applaud enthusiastically. Charlotte smiled proudly at her friend as she came back and sat down beside her.

"You did a *great* job up there," she whispered. "Congratulations!"

Roxanne flushed with pleasure. "I owe it all to you," she whispered back with a sidelong glance, as she relaxed into the seat.

The last speaker was Daniel Tackett. Charlotte listened to him with special interest as he began to talk energetically about his plans for *The Red and the Gold*. In her role as student activities director for the coming year, she knew she'd have to have a close working relationship with Daniel. If the newspaper didn't publicize and support school events, it would be hard to get good turnouts.

Actually, Charlotte was a little worried about just how much support she was going to get from Daniel. He seemed to be a lot more interested in politics than in events. Of course, not all the events she had in mind would be parties — in fact, some activities might even be politically oriented. But if Daniel had the idea that every event she planned was just a lot of frivolous socializing, he might not be very supportive of the kinds of things she was trying to do.

Daniel was almost finished, and Charlotte listened closely. "I want to emphasize the fact that our newspaper has to be open to new ideas and fresh ways of seeing things," he was saying. "There will be a meeting especially for new contributors on the Friday before school starts in the newspaper office. Anybody who wants to join the staff or has some ideas for feature columns should let me have a sample of his or her writing ahead of time. This will give me a chance to recruit new talent, and it'll give interested students a last chance to change their elective to journalism."

Daniel took a deep breath and looked around, pausing to make sure that he had everyone's attention. "Newspapers play a vital role in the life of our country," he went on, raising his voice, "because they give us important information about new ideas and new ways of doing things. *The Red and the Gold* can play just as vital — and exciting — a role in the life of the students of Kennedy High. And if we all are ready to work together, I expect that it will succeed in that role!"

Stirred by Daniel's obviously heartfelt commitment to his task, the audience began to clap. Behind her, Charlotte could hear somebody applauding especially loudly. Curious, she turned to see who it was. A few rows back a pretty, fresh-faced blonde wearing tortoiseshell glasses was sitting on the edge of her seat, clapping her hands enthusiastically. In the seat beside her was a very good-looking boy with a slightly bored, almost disdainful look on his face. It was Torrey Easton, Charlotte saw with surprise.

When the applause for Daniel had died down, the master of ceremonies asked all four speakers to come back up to the front of the room and introduced them once again, saying how proud he was that the Rotary Club could support the plans and dreams of such fine young people. Then, with a final round of applause, the meeting broke up. Several people came up to the front to talk to the speakers. Among them was the pretty blonde girl, who began to talk enthusiastically to Daniel. Charlotte noticed that Torrey Easton was hanging back, as if he didn't want to be a part of the group. Charlotte hoped that Roxanne hadn't noticed her brother, especially since he hadn't taken the trouble to come up and congratulate her.

Charlotte turned to Roxanne, hoping to distract her. "I can't tell you, Rox, how *proud* I am of you!" she exclaimed. "I think you really have a talent for public speaking. You ought to use it more often."

Roxanne smiled. "It's a talent I didn't know I had," she said, "until you helped me to bring it out. But I have to tell the truth, Charlotte, I was really scared up there. Especially when I saw all those cameras. I'm just glad this thing is over, and I don't have to worry about it anymore." Suddenly the smile froze on her face and she just stood there, rooted in place, staring with wide eyes over Charlotte's shoulder.

"What's wrong, Rox?" Charlotte asked. She glanced behind her and then she understood. Vince was standing there, shifting from one foot to the other, looking uncomfortable.

"Uh, hi, Roxanne," Vince said, trying to smile. He turned to Charlotte, and his smile grew broader. "Hi, Charlotte. That was a great speech you made. I really liked the point you made about how important it is for a leader to get *everybody* involved in an activity. Most people seem to just be out to involve their friends and the heck with everybody else. I always feel sorry for the kids who seem to spend most of the time standing on the sidelines, looking on, while everybody else has all the fun."

"Thanks, Vince," Charlotte said happily. That was Vince for you, she told herself, always thinking about the other guy. It was something else to admire him for. But she stopped herself sharply. Vince was Roxanne's boyfriend. She squared her shoulders. "Well," she said, with a meaningful glance at Roxanne. "I have to be going. Call me later, Rox, okay?"

"I will," Roxanne promised. "And thanks again, Char."

Roxanne watched Charlotte walk away, then turned back to Vince.

"I thought you gave a super speech, Vince," she said, hoping her voice didn't sound wobbly. Had there ever been a boy who'd affected her the

86

way Vince did? she wondered. She was shaking, and the tension and uncertainty of not seeing him for the past few weeks was knotting her stomach muscles. She knew she was staring at him, but she couldn't help it. He looked so handsome in his jacket and tie, with his thick dark hair carefully combed.

"Y-you, too, Roxanne," Vince said, fumbling a little bit. He frowned. He'd never given a lot of thought to the way he was going to approach Roxanne, and here he was, about to blow it. And all because Charlotte had been here when he'd first walked up. He'd wanted to talk to her, not Roxanne. But now that he was here, he decided it was a good time to straighten things out between them. He frowned again, trying to remember exactly what he'd planned to say.

"Uh, I'm glad to see that your case of poison ivy's all gone. You look, uh . . . you look terrific. I mean, you can hardly tell that you had a bad case of it." She *did* look terrific, too, he thought to himself. Those eyes of hers were such a fantastic shade of green, almost hypnotizing. He pulled his gaze away, feeling the danger. Just because Roxanne was beautiful on the outside didn't mean that she was beautiful on the inside. He had to remember that.

Roxanne could begin to feel the knot in her stomach relax a little. Vince had said she looked terrific! Maybe he'd gotten over being angry at last. Maybe he was saying that he was ready to forgive her and start over again! She took a deep breath. This was exactly the opportunity she'd been hoping and working toward — an opportunity to apologize and get their relationship back on the right track again, the way it was before everything fell apart.

"Listen, Vince," she said urgently, clenching her fist so hard that the nails bit into her palm, "I want you to know how sorry I am about what happened at camp."

Feeling embarrassed, Vince cleared his throat. "It's okay, you don't have to — " he began.

"But I *want* to," Roxanne went on in a rush. She leaned toward him, looking up at him with the meltingly seductive look that had carried her through so many difficult moments before. "I didn't mean to make you mad at me, honest. In fact, that was the last thing I wanted. I just meant to — "

Vince put a hand on her arm, stopping her. "That's okay, Roxanne," he said quietly. "I don't think I ought to collect any prizes for the way I've acted this summer, either."

There, it was over. It was as much an explanation as he could make. Not an apology, actually, because he didn't think he had anything to apologize for, except to himself. If he hadn't been so idealistic, he would have seen Roxanne for what she really was, instead of for what he wanted her to be. It was a mistake he was never going to make again, with Roxanne or anybody else. And he had to make it clear to her that there wasn't any hope for the two of them — now or ever. He had to put all this behind him and get on with his life.

"Anyway," he hurried on, "it's time that we forgot about all that old stuff in the past and looked at the future. I think that's the best thing for both of us. Don't you agree?"

Roxanne looked up at him eagerly. "Oh, Vince," she breathed in her softest, sexiest voice, "I'm *so* glad to hear you say that!" It was going better — and easier — than she had hoped! He was willing to take part of the blame. And most importantly, he was willing to make a new beginning so that they could be together again! "Yes!" she exclaimed. "We can't go back. We have to set our sights on the future!"

Surprised by Roxanne's unexpected enthusiasm, Vince backed away a little. Somehow he'd thought that she would be more upset by all this, maybe even shed a few tears. He'd seen Roxanne cry before — like that time she'd wrecked her mother's car — and he knew how effective her tears could be. When she cried, she made him feel like a complete jerk. So it was terrific that she was taking everything so well. That made the situation so much easier for both of them. Maybe they could even turn out to be friends, instead of ending up as bitter enemies the way some couples did. Vince began to feel a sense of pride in the two of them. They were doing exactly the right thing, the *civilized* thing.

He grinned warmly. "Well, I guess I'll see you next week, huh? Daniel told me that everybody's planning to go to the state fair the day before school starts. Are you going?"

"Are *you*?" Roxanne countered in a playful,

kittenish tone. Maybe now that they were offi-
cially back together he'd ask her to go to the
fair with him.

But he didn't. He just said, "Yeah, I'm planning to. So I guess I'll see you there." And then,
with a friendly grin, he held out his hand as if
to shake hands. Obviously, even though they were
a couple again, he wanted to keep it cool for a
while.

But Roxanne couldn't help herself. With an
ecstatic smile, she flung her arms around him and
pressed her body close to his. This was the recon-
ciliation she'd been hoping for all these weeks —
she couldn't let it go by without showing him how
glad she was, could she?

Vince hugged Roxanne back, feeling more and
more terrific by the minute. He said good-bye
quickly and left, immensely relieved that he'd
gotten the whole thing over with. Ever since
he'd decided to tell her that they could never go
back together again, he'd been nervous about it,
expecting a bad scene. But Roxanne has been surprisingly calm, even friendly, and her hug had
showed him that she didn't bear any grudges.

His smile of relief broadened to a wide grin as
he began to think about the future. Now that this
unpleasant chore was over and he had done the
right thing, he could get on with his life. And he
had the feeling that his life was about to include
a certain, special girl. A girl who wore soft, lacy
dresses and smelled like old-fashioned lavender
and roses. A girl named Charlotte DeVries.

Chapter
9

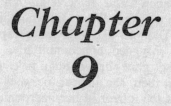

"Torrey?" Sara called.

"Over here," Torrey said, from a chair beside the pool behind the Holiday Inn. There was a bright, round moon overhead, and in its silvery light the nearby trees cast strange, swaying shadows. Sara groped her way through the shadows and sat down beside him, her white cotton shirt a pale blur in the darkness.

"Did you get to talk to Daniel?" Torrey asked. "What did he think of your idea for a movie column?"

"He really liked the idea," Sara said excitedly. "He said it'll fit right into his plan to update *The Red and the Gold* and get more kids to read it on a regular basis." She picked up a leaf from the bench and began to turn it in her fingers. "I really liked Daniel's speech tonight. He's got some great ideas for the paper."

"So what's next?"

"I told him I'd bring him a stack of my movie reviews sometime next week. Then I'll go to the meeting on Friday and see what he thinks about my writing — whether I'm good enough to write for the paper." She glanced at him curiously. "What about you? What did you think of the meeting? Did you like your sister's speech?"

Torrey shrugged noncommittally. Roxanne's speech had gone better than he'd thought it would, but then, she'd spent the week practicing in front of the mirror in her bedroom. As far as the other speeches were concerned — well, he didn't really care. The only one that had interested him at all was Vince's talk about the Rose Hill Volunteer Rescue Squad. Vince had told a couple of good stories about different accident calls the squad had gone on and the way the volunteers had worked together. Torrey was just glad Vince hadn't mentioned any "totaled Mercedes" or "reckless young drivers" in his speech.

"The meeting was okay," he said finally, knowing that Sara was waiting for an answer to her question. "My sister kind of surprised me. I didn't know she had it in her to get up and talk in front of a bunch of people." He glanced at his watch, remembering Sara had said her father was going to pick her up. "What time do you have to meet your dad?"

Now it was Sara's turn to shrug. "Oh, later," she replied. "He said he wouldn't be here right away. He had some stuff to do first. And anyway, this gives us time to talk for a little while. *If* you don't have to get home right away." She hesitated. "Would that be okay?"

Okay? Torrey smiled to himself in the darkness. It was more than okay. It was great, that's what it was. Even though it was a little hard to relate to Sara's starry-eyed enthusiasm sometimes, she was different from any girl he'd ever known. And he couldn't remember liking any other girl half as much as he liked her.

He cleared his throat and edged closer to her on the bench. "Sure it's okay," he said. "I'm glad you're not in a hurry." Torrey swallowed hard. "I mean, it's hard to get to know somebody when you only see them where they work. People are always wandering in and out, and the phone's always ringing."

Sara laughed a little, her voice light. She didn't seem to mind that he was sitting so close to her.

"I know what you mean," she replied. "It's hard enough to know what to say and how to act when you see each other at school or something."

Uneasily, Torrey nodded. Suddenly he wasn't sure he wanted Sara to know what he was really like. What if she found out that he hung out at the Hall of Shame and that his whole life was a screwed-up mess? She'd never like him if she knew. Warily, he said, "Maybe it won't be worth the effort to learn about me. Maybe you'll find out you really hate me."

"No," she said, "it's *always* worth the effort to get to know somebody." She half-turned on the bench to face him, and there was another silence.

Then she added, almost in a whisper, "Especially if it's somebody you already like a lot." Her voice trembled a little.

At Sara's words, something inside Torrey began to relax, like a spring uncoiling. He felt suddenly lighter and less afraid. "Yeah," he said finally, "I guess you're right."

"You know, I never thought about it before this minute," Sara said slowly, looking up at the moon, "but you can never really tell another person anything important about your life. All the important things are buried deep down, underneath. What you end up telling is just the superficial stuff, stuff that doesn't matter a whole lot anyway."

Torrey laughed. "So let's talk about superficial stuff," he said. And then he felt embarrassed. He hadn't meant to sound so flip. He didn't want to know superficial things about Sara — he wanted to know *important* things, *deep* things.

Sara turned to look at him, her face serene in the moonlight, her lips parted to speak. Torrey felt a surge of emotions well up inside him. He moved his hand gently to her cheek, and he put his arm around her shoulders, pulling her closer to him. For a long moment they looked at each other, and then he bent to kiss her. They were both stiff at first, uncertain. But then, tentatively, Sara put her arms around his neck and melted into his arms. Torrey held her tightly, feeling dizzy with happiness.

For a long time they sat on the shadowy bench,

clinging to one another. Then Torrey pulled back a little, tracing the curve of Sara's cheekbone with the tip of his finger.

"Listen, uh," he began with a small laugh, "aren't you afraid your dad is going to wonder where you are? I mean, I don't want to get you into trouble or anything."

Sara dropped her arms and ran her fingers nervously through her hair. "Yeah, I guess it's probably time for me to go," she said, sounding reluctant to leave. "Dad's probably out front by now, or else he'll be here soon."

She had suddenly changed, Torrey thought curiously. A minute before, she had been warm and relaxed in his arms. Now her face was taut with worry and her voice was strained.

"I'll walk you," Torrey offered lamely. He wished he could think of something else to say.

Sara stood up quickly. "No, that's okay. I'll be fine by myself," she said. "In fact, it would probably be a good idea if you just went home. Dad might uh . . . he might get mad if he saw us together."

"Well, okay," Torrey said, still wondering what had upset her. He was about to leave, but something stopped him. He turned to face her, putting his hand on her shoulder. "Sara, is something the matter? Did I do something wrong?"

Sara shook her head, not looking at him. "No," she murmured. "It's nothing, really. I . . . I just have to leave, that's all."

Torrey searched her face, trying to figure out why she'd become so distant. Was it somehow his fault? He didn't know. "When can I see you again?" he finally asked.

Sara pulled away. "I . . . I'm not sure," she said. She was being strangely evasive. "Why don't you come by the store?"

"That's not what I meant," Torrey said. "I mean, when can we get together, just the two of us, alone?"

"I don't know!" Sara flared. Then she turned on her heel and walked quickly, almost running, toward the front of the building.

For a minute or two, Torrey stood there, staring after her, thinking, his eyebrows knit together in a puzzled frown. Then he went to his bike and began to unlock it from the bicycle rack, his thoughts racing. Why had she changed so suddenly? And why had she said her dad might get mad if he saw the two of them together? If he was the wonderful pal Sara claimed he was, wouldn't he be happy for her? And if he was devoted to her, how come he hadn't picked her up right after the meeting ended? Why would he make her wait for almost an hour?

His mind still full of unanswered questions, Torrey climbed on his bike and began to pedal down the street toward home. Then he saw something that shocked him so much, he almost crashed his bike into the utility pole at the corner. It was Sara, her blouse a white blur in the shadows. She was jogging along the dark sidewalk, all by herself!

For a second, Torrey didn't know what to do. What had happened? Had she and her father got-

96

ten into an argument? Or maybe her father hadn't been there, and she'd decided to walk home alone. Whatever happened, it definitely wasn't a good idea for a girl to be out by herself this late at night, even in Rose Hill. As she turned a corner and began to jog up a side street, Torrey turned, too, keeping about a block behind her but at the same time making sure that she was always in sight. He'd see her safely home, Torrey decided, and then he'd ride on, without letting her know that he'd followed her.

From what Sara had said about her father not being able to keep a job, Torrey had figured they lived in a small tract house or maybe an apartment. So it was a major shock when he saw where she was headed. The neighborhood she was heading into was an expensive neighborhood, filled with elegant town houses set behind sloping, park-like lawns, not unlike the kind that the Eastons lived in. Just then, Sara turned and walked up the steps in front of one of the town houses. Torrey stopped and hid his bike behind a small clump of trees at the curb, then watched as Sara began to knock on the front door.

"Dad, let me in," she called softly, between knocks. "It's Sara. I'm home."

As Torrey watched, his mouth gaping open, she knocked again, louder. When there was no answer, she hit the door with her fist in angry frustration. "Dad," she called, hitting the door again, "let me in!" Clumsily she began to search through her purse for her key.

Torrey couldn't watch any longer. He had to

find out what was going on. He laid his bike at the curb and ran up the walk, his tennis shoes not making a sound on the pavement. He could see now why Sara hadn't been able to find her key. She was crying. A tear had splashed from her cheek onto her hand.

"Sara?" he said. "What's wrong?"

Sara whirled to face him. "Torrey!" she gasped, her face going even more pale in the thin stream of moonlight. In her surprise she dropped her purse onto the concrete step, her wallet and keys spilling out. "What are you doing here?"

"I saw you walking home, and I followed you," Torrey said. "I was worried." He bent over to scoop up her purse and handed it to her. "What's the matter? Did something happen to your dad? Or. . . . " He paused, staring at her frightened face. He was suddenly struck by a new idea. "Or wasn't he going to pick you up in the first place?"

Her quick, sharp breath told Torrey the truth. He could also see it in her eyes, behind the tears she was trying to blink away.

"You lied to me!" he exclaimed in surprise. "But why? Why, Sara?"

"No, I didn't lie," she insisted, brushing a tear from her cheek. "I don't know what you're talking about." She bent back to her purse and clutched her keys in her hand. "Dad couldn't come to pick me up, that's all. There was. . . . " She hesitated, then spoke quickly. "There was an emergency. He had to take a friend to the hospital, and he's going to be stuck there all night. He phoned and left a message for me at the hotel registration desk. I didn't have the money for a taxi, so I jogged home by myself." She stared back at him defensively, straightening her shoulders. "I can get around by myself. You don't have to look out for me."

"But if your dad's at the hospital, how come you were calling for him when you knocked on the door?" Torrey asked. "And how come you live in such a fancy town house when you told me your father couldn't hold down a job?" He nodded at the house. "I mean, people can't afford to live in places like this on a part-time paycheck."

Sara backed up against the door, the tears welling up in her blue eyes. "I don't know." She swallowed hard, starting to sob. "I wish you'd just go away. Just go home and leave me alone!"

Torrey planted himself squarely in front of her. "I'm not going home," he said, folding his arms across his chest. "Not until you tell me what this is all about."

"I don't have to tell you anything," Sara said angrily, clenching her small fists. "You can't order me around. And you don't have any right to follow me."

"Maybe not, but I'm not leaving until I get some answers." He gestured toward the door. "Why don't we go inside where we can be more comfortable?" He raised his hand toward the doorbell, about to press it.

"No, no!" Sara exclaimed, catching his arm before he could push the button. "You can't go inside." She sighed and dropped both hands to her sides, helplessly. "Okay," she said in a whisper, "so I didn't tell you the truth. So I lied to you." She looked down. Another tear splashed on her hand.

Torrey waited a minute, but she didn't go on. "Lied about what?" he prompted.

"About . . . about my father," Sara said miserably.

"You mean, you *don't* live with him?" Torrey asked in confusion.

"No, I do," Sara said. "Only it's not the way I told you. I mean, he isn't a charmer and a softie, like the father in *Pretty in Pink*. He isn't my buddy, either. I wish he were, but he isn't." She wiped her eyes with the sleeve of her shirt. "We don't go to museums or the zoo, or sit around and watch TV together. He doesn't have time for any of that stuff."

"What's he like, then?" Torrey asked, bewildered. "He doesn't . . . he doesn't treat you badly, does he?"

Sara shook her head wearily. "No, it's nothing like that. But he's not home very much, so we don't have time to do things together. He's a stockbroker, and he's always at the office, or entertaining clients, or trying to put a new project together."

"Oh," Torrey said, suddenly understanding. "You mean, he's a workaholic." *That* he knew about. His own father was always too busy with work to see either him or Roxanne very often. Even when they had all lived together, they hardly saw him. He was always at the office.

100

Sara nodded, still not looking at Torrey. She sniffled. "When he *is* home, which isn't very often, he drinks a lot." She hesitated, and then added, very softly, "He usually drinks until he falls asleep."

Now Torrey understood the glimpses of pain he had seen in Sara's eyes. He understood the frustrated anger he had seen when she was beating on the door with her fist. But even though he knew those things about her, he still cared for her, maybe even more than he had before. He felt closer to her now than he had earlier, when he was holding her in his arms. Frustration, disappointment, rejection — they were all emotions *he* had felt, too. He felt them every day just trying to cope with his family. The strange sense of kinship he had felt with Sara that day at the Video Stop now made perfect sense to him. The two of them *did* share a bond — a really important and meaningful bond.

"Listen, Sara," he began, "I want to — "

"No, Torrey," Sara said. She turned away from him, struggling to keep from crying. "So now you know the truth. You know what I'm really like. It isn't the way you thought. *I'm* not the way you thought. I'm not the sweet, innocent little girl I sometimes seem to be."

Torrey put his finger under her chin and raised it so that she had to look into his eyes. "I do know what you're like," he said wonderingly. "Inside, you're angry all the time, aren't you? And it hurts, too, doesn't it? Every time he promises you something and doesn't come through, every time — "

Sara pulled away and put her hands over her ears. "I don't want to hear this, Torrey," she cried. "Stop!"

But Torrey didn't stop. The words just kept on coming and coming, as if there was a lake of feelings all dammed up inside him and the dam had just burst. "And you keep wondering what you did to deserve such a lousy deal, don't you? And you wonder whether it's *your* fault that things are the way they are — "

"You've *got* to leave, now," Sara said urgently. "Please, just leave!"

Torrey stared at her. "You don't mean that," he said.

"Yes, I do," Sara insisted. She turned away, but Torrey saw the glint of fresh tears on her cheek. "I can't see you ever again."

"Why? Is it because you lied? Sara, I don't care about that — "

"Just go!" Sara burst out angrily. "Stop trying to make me feel better. It was wrong of me to ever get involved with you, and I just want you to leave."

Torrey took her shoulders in his hands and shook her gently. "Sara whatever you do, *don't* say we can't see each other," he said. He could hear the pleading note in his voice, but he didn't make any effort to hide it. "Maybe I can help; maybe together we can both help each other. I don't care where it is, I'll meet you anywhere you say — at the Video Stop or the drugstore. Even at that newspaper meeting you were talking about." He swallowed. "I'll — I'll even write something to try to get on the paper, too."

Sara pulled away and began to search in her purse. After a minute she found her key and held it tightly in her hand.

"No, Torrey," she said. Her voice was calmer now, determined. "I've made up my mind. I'm not going to that newspaper meeting on Friday. It was stupid of me to even think I could be a writer. And it was stupid of me to think things could ever work out for us."

"Wait! Sara!" Torrey said, putting out his hand. "Please, don't go!"

But Sara didn't answer. She opened the door and slipped inside. Before she closed it, however, Torrey caught a glimpse of the living room. He saw her father, in a white shirt with his sleeves rolled up and his tie loosened, asleep on the living room sofa. Then Sara slammed the door in his face, and Torrey was left alone in the quiet moonlight.

Chapter
10

"What do you think of this outfit?" Charlotte
asked, holding up a baby blue hip-length sweater
and a slim gray flannel skirt for her mother to
look at. The two of them were in Charlotte's
bedroom, going through her closet to make sure
Charlotte had everything she needed for school.
She had learned a long time ago that you got the
maximum mileage out of your wardrobe if you
planned your clothes combinations carefully.
That way, you didn't have to wear the same outfit
very often. Of course, wearing the same thing day
after day wasn't *really* a problem given the size of
her clothes allowance. But then, Charlotte always
liked to have things planned out ahead of time.
You never knew what might come up, and it
always paid to be prepared.

"The blue and gray look wonderful together,

honey," Mrs. DeVries said, in her warm southern accent. "And the blue is such a good color on you. But what about adding something with a little spark to it? The combination might just be a little bland, don't you think?"

"You're right," Charlotte said. She turned and pulled a bright blue and green scarf out of her drawer. "How about this? Better?"

"It's perfect!" Mrs. DeVries exclaimed. "You can wear blue or gray stockings."

"Yes, and my new black flats," Charlotte said. "The outfit won't be bland after all." She grinned and opened her closet door. "Did I show you my new blouse? I got it last week." She held up a soft yellow long-sleeved blouse with ruffles at the throat. "It exactly matches the yellow in my blue-and-yellow skirt. And I have a pair of blue shoes — a darker blue, but it's still a good match."

Mrs. DeVries, as slim and blonde as her daughter, leaned back in the pink upholstered chair. "You have an artist's eye for color, Charlotte," she said. "And a great figure for clothes, too. You're so much prettier — not to mention more together — than I was at your age."

Charlotte flopped down on her bed and blew a stray wisp of hair out of her eyes. "Prettier?" she said, rolling her eyes meaningfully. "I've seen the pictures of you, remember? That one of you in your blue prom formal, with the flowers in your hair? That's my favorite. You looked so beautiful and so happy."

Mrs. DeVries smiled. "I *was* happy that night,"

she said reminiscently. "I went to the prom with Jim Neal. We'd gone steady for almost two years, and I was sure that he was going to give me a ring for graduation."

"A ring?" Charlotte gave her mother a quick look. "You never told me about that! Who was Jim Neal?"

A tender smile tugged at Mrs. DeVries's lips. "I didn't? Oh, Jim was the most wonderful boy. He was so much fun, always laughing, always ready for a good time. I was convinced I loved him."

"But if you loved him . . ." Charlotte began.

Mrs. DeVries shook her head. "I didn't. Not really. Anyway, he went to Georgia Tech and I went to Sophie Newcomb College, and a few months later I met your father. Then I found out what love was *really* about." She leaned forward and took Charlotte's hand. "Which just goes to show you, honey, that what sometimes feels like love isn't always real love. First love especially can be wonderful and thrilling — and painful. It's sort of like learning how to ride a bike; one minute you're sailing along, feeling the wind in your face and a glorious feeling of freedom, and the next minute you're sailing into the neighbor's rosebush."

Charlotte looked at her mother. "You know," she said, "I wish Roxanne could talk to you. Maybe it would make her feel better about this thing with Vince. I think she's got a bad case of first love, and she hurts terribly."

"Roxanne." Mrs. DeVries's face took on a

thoughtful look. "You know, I would like to be able to talk to her, too, if it would help. But I have a feeling that it's hard for Roxanne to share her feelings with anyone. She always looks so defensive, so wary." Mrs. DeVries shook her head.

Charlotte nodded and smiled sadly. "You know," she said, "I think you might be right about Roxanne. She laughs and jokes all the time, but I have the feeling that deep down she's really different. She's angry and afraid. Maybe it's got something to do with her family. Her mother isn't at all like you, Mom. She's — "

The telephone on Charlotte's night table began to ring, interrupting her. As she reached for it, her mother stood up and went to the door. "It's time for me to do something about dinner." She smiled warmly at Charlotte. "I'll be down in the kitchen if you want me for anything."

"Okay," Charlotte said, waving, as her mother went out the door. "Hello," she said eagerly into receiver. It was probably Roxanne, with a report on what had happened the night before. Charlotte had expected her to call early this morning, and she'd been a little puzzled when she hadn't heard anything.

"Hi, Charlotte," came a deep male voice. "It's Vince."

Charlotte's heart seemed to stop for an instant. "Vince," she said hesitantly. Why was *Vince* calling *her*?

"Yeah, Vince DiMase. I . . . I was just calling to say hi and see how you are."

"Oh, well, uh, hi." Charlotte said. She bit her

lip. She could hear the tension in her voice, and she wondered if Vince could hear it, too. "I'm fine," she said uncertainly. "How are you?"

"I'm fine," Vince said. There was a pause, and then he laughed a little. It was a shy but natural laugh. "Well," he said, "now that we know we're both fine, I guess I can tell you why I called. I was thinking about the state fair next week. Somebody said it was your idea for the crowd to all meet there."

Charlotte laughed, too, feeling a little more at ease. "Well, actually I had been thinking of having a big party — you know, kind of a fare-well-to-summer party here at my house. But then it dawned on me that if we went to the fair instead, there'd be merry-go-rounds and Ferris wheels and bumper cars — we don't have any of those things at my house."

Vince laughed again, a husky, throaty laugh that made Charlotte's pulse race. "It sounds like a terrific idea — something definitely worthy of our new student activities director." He paused. "Listen, I was wondering. Would you want to go with me to the fair?"

For a second, Charlotte thought that perhaps she hadn't heard him correctly. "You mean, as your date?" Did this mean that Vince was through with Roxanne? From everything she'd seen while they were at leadership camp, she had suspected that Roxanne might not be able to get him back. But she also knew that Roxanne was still crazy about him and was still determined to win him back.

"I could pick you up in the middle of the afternoon," Vince was saying. "I hear there's a square dance that afternoon, and I thought it might be fun to. . . . "

Charlotte held the receiver away from her ear and stared indecisively at it. What should she say? She really liked Vince — more than she wanted to admit, probably. And she knew he was so straightforward and honest. He wouldn't be asking her for a date if he hadn't completely ended his relationship with Roxanne, at least as far as he was concerned.

But on the other hand, Charlotte thought, there were Roxanne's feelings to consider. If she went to the fair with Vince, Roxanne would almost surely feel hurt and angry — and she'd have a right to feel that way. Roxanne was her friend, probably her closest friend here in Rose Hill. Charlotte couldn't intentionally hurt anybody — and *especially* not a friend.

Charlotte took a deep breath. "I'm sorry, Vince," she said, as coolly as she could manage, "but I've already made plans for the fair. I'm going with Roxanne."

"Oh," Vince said. "I see." There was another silence. "Has . . . has Roxanne told you about our conversation last night?" he asked finally. "You see, we — "

"No, I haven't talked to her today," Charlotte interrupted, hoping her voice sounded more firm and steady than it felt. "But it wouldn't make any difference what you talked about. I've already made my plans. But it was really nice of you to

109

ask," she added politely. "I'm sure I'll see you there, with the rest of the crowd."

"Okay, sure," Vince said. She could hear the disappointment in his voice. "Listen," he said, "if you change your mind, will you let me know?"

"Of course," Charlotte said.

After they had said good-bye and hung up, Charlotte sat on her bed for a long time, staring out the window and turning things over in her mind. Finally she got up and went downstairs to the kitchen, where her mother was putting a chocolate cake in the oven.

Charlotte sat down on a kitchen stool and cupped her chin in her hands on the counter, watching in silence as her mother washed salad greens and sliced tomatoes in the pleasant, cheerful kitchen. Mrs. DeVries loved to cook, and her kitchen was hung with gleaming copper pans and cooking utensils.

"Something on your mind?" Mrs. DeVries said finally, into the silence. She finished with the tomato and reached for an onion.

Charlotte looked up. "That was Vince DiMase on the phone a little while ago," she said. "You know, the guy Roxanne was going with earlier this summer."

Mrs. DeVries nodded. "Didn't you tell me that they had stopped seeing one another?" she asked as she began to slice a red onion into delicate rings.

"Yes, they broke up sometime in July." Charlotte picked up a white paper napkin and began to flute it in her fingers, making a delicate little fan. "But even though Vince seems to think that it's all over, Roxanne hasn't given up yet — or at least, she hadn't as of last night when we talked about it. She's been desperately hoping that he'll change his mind and get back together with her." Charlotte looked at her mother searchingly. "The problem is, he called me to ask if I'd go to the fair with him."

Her mother put down the knife and looked at Charlotte. "I see. What did you tell him?"

Charlotte sighed. "I told him that I had already made plans to go with Roxanne." Absently, she began to fan herself with the folded napkin. "I felt really *torn* about it, though. On the one hand, I wanted to go to the fair with him, and I certainly didn't want to hurt his feelings or make him feel as if I don't like him. That would be a lie. I *do* like him." She sighed again. "But on the other hand, I didn't think it was fair to Roxanne to accept his invitation. I mean, she's my *friend*, and I couldn't play that kind of dirty trick on her. I would feel terrible if I'd been involved with somebody and Roxanne started going out with him when she knew that I still liked him."

Mrs. DeVries smiled, her face full of sympathy. "I imagine you would," she said. "You'd probably feel angry and bitter, too. And I'm very glad that you took the time to consider how Roxanne would feel before you thought about what *you* wanted to do. It must have been a hard decision to make."

"Do you think I did the right thing?" Charlotte asked hesitantly. "Vince is a very nice boy. I hope I didn't hurt *his* feelings." She sighed. "I guess I felt as if I was going to hurt somebody, no matter what I said. Maybe even me."

"I'm sure you did the right thing," her mother assured her. "Roxanne is your friend, and your loyalty to her is very important. And if Vince is as nice as you say he is, he'll know why you had to turn him down. And he'll respect you for your decision." She came over and put her arm around Charlotte's shoulders. "It must have been a hard thing to do, and I'm very proud of you, honey."

Charlotte let out a long breath and hugged her mother back. "Thanks, Mom," she said. "What would I do without you?"

But even though she was glad that her mother approved of what she had done, she couldn't quite get the sound of Vince's disappointed voice out of her ears. And she couldn't forget her *own* disappointment, either.

Chapter
11

Torrey ambled into the kitchen on Friday morning and turned the radio on to his favorite rock station. Then he took a cereal box out of the cupboard and shook it. It sounded almost empty, but there was probably enough for one more bowl. He poured what was left into a bowl, added milk, and took it to the kitchen counter to eat. Looking out the kitchen window, he saw it was a gray and gloomy day outside, and it was beginning to drizzle. The weather matched his mood exactly.

Torrey was still mulling over what had happened on Sara's front steps a few nights before. What was worse, he was beginning to feel really upset about the possibility of not seeing Sara again. Since he'd met her, his life had changed. For one thing, she'd introduced him to the thrill of biking. But it was more than just biking, much more. She'd also shown him that you could always find something in life worth doing, something to look forward to in the midst of all the dreary sameness. If he lost her, he'd go back to being his old self, to being the old aimless, drifting Torrey. There wouldn't be anything special to live for anymore. His life would go down the tubes — back to what it always was.

Suddenly, the music stopped and Torrey turned around. It was Roxanne, her blue robe wrapped around her. Her tawny red hair was a mess, and her eyes were red and puffy. The blotchy eyes were a total giveaway. She'd probably been crying about Vince again. Of course, she had never talked to Torrey about it — she didn't exactly talk to him about things like that — but he'd heard rumors that Vince had broken up with her, and it was obvious that something was wrong. For once, Torrey could almost sympathize with the old dragon woman. After what had happened with Sara the other night, he thought he knew how Roxanne must be feeling. So to be nice, he didn't say anything about the fact that Roxanne had turned off the radio while Iron Alloy, his favorite band, was playing.

Roxanne opened the refrigerator. "I don't know how you can stand that awful racket at this hour of the morning," she grumbled, looking for the milk. "And how you can call it music is beyond me."

"It's not so early," Torrey pointed out, in a reasonable tone. "It's after ten."

"And I suppose you've already been for a bike

ride," Roxanne snapped, taking the milk out. "What have you turned over, a new leaf or something — getting your predawn exercise, even in the rain? What are you trying to do, get in condition for the Olympics?"

Without saying anything, Torrey turned back to his cereal. He didn't want to get into a stupid fight with Roxanne this morning. He had more important things on his mind. Today was Friday, the day that Daniel Tackett was holding his meeting for new newspaper writers. Torrey knew he had to try to figure out a way to get Sara to the meeting, even though she'd said she wasn't going to go.

Roxanne put the milk on the counter and got a bowl from the cupboard. She sat down on a stool next to Torrey and reached for the cereal box.

Torrey looked up. "We're out of cereal," he said absently, still thinking about Sara.

"Out of cereal?" Roxanne asked angrily. She shook the box. "You mean you pigged out on it, that's what you mean. You ate what you wanted and you didn't leave any for the rest of us!"

"There was only enough for one bowl," Torrey said, taking his dish to the sink to rinse it out.

"That's just like you," Roxanne stormed. "Always thinking of yourself, never thinking of anyone else." She stood up. "*Nobody* in this house ever thinks of anybody else!"

Torrey turned around, drying his hands. "Listen, Rox, I'm sorry about the cereal," he said mildly, "but it's no big deal. There's plenty of bread, and I saw a jar of jam in the refrigerator. Why don't you make some toast or something?"

"No big deal?" Roxanne cried. "You're not the one who doesn't get any cereal. Who are *you* to say it's no big deal?"

Suddenly, a new voice broke into the argument.

"Don't you two have *any* consideration for other people? I was up very late last night, and I didn't plan to get up until noon. But who can sleep with you two bickering like a pair of five-year-olds? I could hear you all the way upstairs."

Torrey looked up. It was his mother, still in her nightgown, pushing the hair out of her eyes and heading for the coffeepot.

"Sorry, Mom," he muttered.

Roxanne stared at him. "Sorry? You're never sorry, for *anything*," she cried, and ran out of the kitchen.

With a long sigh, Torrey went to the window and stood there for a minute, looking out at the drizzle. Then, with sudden determination, he grabbed his leather jacket and headed for the garage to get his bike. Rain or no rain, he *had* to talk to Sara. And he had to talk to her *now*. He couldn't put it off.

Torrey knocked again, harder. The drizzle had almost stopped, and he shook the rain out of his damp hair. He waited a moment, and then raised his hand to knock again. But just at that moment, the door opened, and he saw Sara standing in front of him.

"Sara, I —" Torrey began. But Sara didn't give him a chance to speak. Swiftly, without saying a word, she started to shut the door in his face. Torrey immediately stuck his sneaker into the doorway, keeping the door from closing.

"I don't want to see you," Sara said, her voice muffled. She pushed the door against his foot. "I don't want to *talk* to you, either. Go away."

"I won't go away," Torrey replied calmly. "Not until we've had a chance to talk."

"There's nothing to discuss."

"There's *plenty* to discuss," Torrey said, shifting his weight to keep the door from pinching his foot. "I know exactly how you feel — how angry you are at your dad, how angry you are at *yourself*." He took a deep breath. For the first time since he could remember, he wasn't trying to play it cool. He wasn't making any attempt to hide his feelings or to keep them from showing in his voice. "I know how you feel because I've been there myself," he said. "That's what I want to talk about."

There was a moment of silence, and then Sara opened the door. "You can come in. For a few minutes, anyway," she said reluctantly. "And you can talk. But that doesn't mean I have to listen. And you're not going to change my mind about anything. It's already made up."

She went into the living room, and Torrey followed her. She sat down on one end of the sofa, and he sat on the other. She was wearing jeans and a baggy man's shirt with a smear of blue paint on the sleeve, and she hadn't combed her hair.

117

But he liked the way it hung around her face in a tousled mass instead of being neatly brushed and smoothed back. She looked vulnerable, like a little girl — an extremely sad little girl. Torrey felt his throat go dry. More than anything else, he didn't want Sara to get hurt the way *he* had been hurt. She was too sweet and good for that.

Torrey sat on the edge of the sofa and leaned forward. "I've been thinking a lot about what happened the other night," he said urgently. "And what I want to tell you is that you can't give up. You can't stop trying, the way I have."

Sara looked at him, obviously listening in spite of herself. "Give up?" she asked.

"Yeah. A long time ago, I decided that it was hopeless to try to change the things that were screwed-up in my life. I mean, I couldn't make my mom care about me, so why try? Same with my dad. So I. . . . "

He shifted uncomfortably. It was hard — *very* hard — to tell Sara how he felt. He'd never put these feelings into words before, much less said them out loud to someone he barely knew. But he had to take the risk. He had to tell her and make her understand that if she didn't stay involved, if she let herself be defeated by her problems with her dad, the pain would only get worse.

"So I just gave up," he said. "I started hanging out with a pretty weird bunch of people over at the Hall of Fame, people who drink and get into trouble sometimes. They at least accepted me. And why shouldn't they? We were all a bunch of losers. School was a total wipeout — the teachers and even the other kids treated me like a punk. All I could think about was getting in a car and driving it as fast as it would go, anywhere — the farther the better. I gave up trying to do anything worthwhile because I hated everybody. Nobody cared about me."

Sara looked as if she were going to say something, but Torrey held up his hand. He had to finish this. If he stopped now, he might not be able to get up the nerve to start again.

"Then I met you," he said, "and things are changing for me. You're so enthusiastic about the things you're doing — your film reviews and your work at the Video Stop — and you've shown me what it's like to really feel interested in the world. Anyway, what I'm saying is, I don't want you to give up the way *I* did, because I can't stand the thought of the bad things that have happened to me happening to you. You've got to be brave and face up to disappointments, even when they hurt so bad that you think you can't stand it anymore." He swallowed hard, willing her to understand what he was trying to tell her. "I guess what I'm saying is, I need you, Sara. I need you to help me get back into the world, help me get going again."

Sara looked down at her hands, which were twisted in her lap. "But don't you see?" she asked, almost whispering "I *lied* . . . I *lied*. I lied to you, and that was bad enough. But I've been lying to myself for a long time. And I can't face you, knowing you know the truth." She shivered and her eyes filled with tears.

"But you lied for a reason," Torrey pointed out. "You didn't lie just for the fun of it, or to get something for yourself. You lied because . . . because you were afraid."

Sara looked up at him, her blue eyes filled with so much pain, so much sadness, that Torrey's throat tightened.

"Yes, but there's more to it than that," she said. "I don't want to be with you because" — she swallowed hard — "because you know about all the things I hate about my life. With you, I'd never be able to forget about those things, even for a little while."

"Is that so bad?" Torrey asked. "You've made me see things about myself that *I* needed to see."

For a moment, Sara was silent, an indecisive look on her face. Then she spoke quietly, almost as if she were talking to herself. "After Mom left and Dad started working so much of the time, everything was so awful that I just couldn't . . . I couldn't even *think* about it." She looked back down at her hands again, her fingers twisting her shirttail. "So I'd watch a movie and imagine I was *living* it, because the movie was so much better than my life. The movies always had a happy ending, but me — "

She broke off, and there was silence for a minute. Finally, she said, her voice breaking, "I could see that my life wasn't ever going to have a happy ending. It was empty — so completely, utterly empty."

Torrey leaned toward her and reached for her

hand. "But if we were together," he said quietly, "maybe it wouldn't be empty anymore."

She stared at him.

"I mean," Torrey said slowly, trying hard to choose exactly the right words. "I know I'm not the kind of guy you might have been looking for. I don't do well in school the way you do, and I'm not popular with the other kids like the guys that Roxanne runs around with. But if you want me to be, I can promise to *be* there for you when you need me."

Suddenly Sara's blue eyes were bright with tears and the corners of her mouth began to tremble. She pulled her hand away and fished for a tissue in the pocket of her shirt.

"Oh, hey!" Torrey said, feeling miserable. "I didn't mean to make you cry. I'm sorry." He moved toward her on the sofa, his fingers aching to brush away her tears. "I'm really sorry," he repeated.

"It's not you," Sara said, wiping her eyes. "I mean, I'm not crying because you upset me. It's just that I never had anybody say anything like that to me before."

Torrey looked at her. "Then you'll think about it?" he asked hopefully. "You won't give up!"

Sara put down her tissue. "I don't have to think about it," she said softly, her eyes fixed on his. "I won't give up. Not ever."

The world seemed to stop for Torrey. "You *mean* that?" he asked.

The tears were still trembling on Sara's lashes,

but she was smiling now. Torrey thought she looked more beautiful than ever. "I really mean that," she said. "I mean it with all my heart." And then he pulled her to him and kissed her, very gently, feeling the warmth of her arms creeping around his neck.

After a minute he pulled back a little. "Well, then," he said with a smile, "now that we've got that settled, I guess we ought to talk about this afternoon."

"This afternoon?" Sara asked. There was a sharp edge to her voice.

"Yeah. It's Friday, remember. *The Red and the Gold* meeting?"

At that, Sara shrank back. "That's all off," she said glumly. "There's no point in going to the meeting. I decided not to take my reviews to Daniel."

Torrey grinned. "Yeah, I figured you might not submit them," he said. "That's why *I* took them in."

"You did what?" Sara asked unbelievingly, her eyes widening. "You turned my movie reviews in to Daniel Tackett without telling me?"

Torrey nodded, watching to make sure she wasn't going to be angry. "I went by the Video Stop the other day when you weren't there, and I made copies of a half-dozen of your reviews. I dropped them off with Daniel yesterday." His grin got broader and a little embarrassed. "I even wrote a piece myself about biking, and I left that with him, too. I know it's not very good, but at least I tried."

"You did all that for me?" Sara said softly.

"Yeah," Torrey said. "For you. So how about it? I'll go to the meeting if you will."

Suddenly Sara threw her arms around his neck. "I'll go, she said happily, "if *you'll* go."

Outdoors, the sun suddenly broke through the clouds and flooded the day with a warm, bright light.

Chapter
12

Daniel Tackett sat down in the small dining alcove and stared at the stack of papers in front of him on the table. It had been raining all morning, but the sun had just come out, and the sky was looking brighter. Maybe it wasn't going to be such a bad day after all. He took a sip of the lemonade his mother had made for him before she went to work and pulled the top set of papers toward him. If he was going to give everybody thoughtful comments on their work at the newspaper meeting this afternoon, he'd better get busy reading the writing samples that had been turned in to him during the week.

The first paper-clipped set of papers was from a sophomore who wanted to be a sportswriter. He'd handed in two different pieces: One was on the last football game of the previous season, and the other was a feature on JFK's star pitcher. Daniel read both, frowning a little, and then he read them again, more slowly this time, concentrating on what he was reading. Everything was accurate, but there was something missing. The writing didn't have any *life*, it didn't have any vitality. If you were going to cover sports, you had to be able to make your readers feel as though they were actually *at* the game, make them *feel* the excitement. You had to haul them out onto the field beside the players, right in the middle of the play. This kid, even though he knew how to put the words down on paper, didn't know how to grab his readers. Daniel sighed and put the boy's work to one side. Sports coverage in *The Red and the Gold* was important — too important to hand it to somebody who'd just cover the games and write up a dry report.

The second and third submissions Daniel read were much easier to deal with. One was from a girl who wanted to write a gossip column, and Daniel had to admit that even though he didn't have much use for the kind of trash usually found in columns like that, she'd probably do a pretty good job. Emily Stevens had handled a similar column last year, but this one was even better; spicier, Daniel thought. She had a bright, chatty, *acidic* style that belonged in a gossip column, as well as a nose for the kind of interesting personal tidbits that would attract readers. He grinned. Take her short item about the romance between Vince DiMase and Roxanne Easton, for instance:

"The grapevine has it that Rose Hill's one-man rescue squad, Vince DiMase, and

Foxy Rox Easton finally called it quits during leadership camp this summer, after Roxanne took a nosedive into a poison-ivy patch. Apparently, this was one time when Vince decided not to play the knight-in-shining-armor and rescue the pretty princess from her dire distress. Better luck next time, Rox, honey. We hope you'll find another hero around the next corner. As for you, Vince, we'll all be waiting breathlessly to see what new princess will fall at your feet."

Daniel couldn't help laughing in spite of himself. Even though he thought it was silly and trivial, it was exactly the stuff that kept readers — even Daniel had to admit that everyone likes a little trash once in a while — coming back for more. And the writer *was* perceptive, there was no doubt about it. All that stuff about Vince being a one-man rescue squad was right on the mark. And where had she heard about Roxanne's poison ivy? Roxanne had been so careful to stay out of sight while her rash was still visible. Daniel chuckled again as he put the papers aside.

The third piece was just as easy to deal with. Surprisingly, it was from Torrey Easton, Roxanne's kid brother. Daniel didn't know much about him, even though he'd also gone to Stevenson, because Torrey was a couple of years younger. And Torrey certainly wouldn't hang out with Daniel's crowd — Torrey hung out at the Hall of Shame with a bunch of derelicts like himself. Rumor had it that Torrey'd come close to getting kicked out of school a couple of times. If Daniel had been asked to guess what the little wayward Easton was interested in, he would have said fast cars and heavy metal rock. But the piece he'd submitted was about bikes and how it felt to do long-distance riding. In a way, Daniel thought, it wasn't a bad piece, because you could sort of get a feel for what the kid was trying to say. He'd put some heart into it, there was no question about that, and it was clear that he was really into bicycle racing. But there were major problems with Torrey's spelling and grammar. Daniel shook his head, studying the piece. If Torrey Easton wanted to write for *The Red and the Gold*, he was going to have to find a very good tutor. And Daniel doubted that Torrey cared enough about writing — or anything — to go to that kind of trouble. Daniel looked at the paper for a minute. He really ought to mark it up, just to show Torrey how many errors there were. But if the kid saw all that red ink, he'd probably be pretty demoralized. Daniel put the piece on the "reject" pile, along with the offerings from the would-be sportswriter.

The sun was shining in earnest now, and the puddles on the small concrete patio outside the window were already beginning to dry up. Suddenly — maybe it was a trick of the light, or the way the sun touched the leaves of the trees at the back of the lot — Daniel thought of Lin. At leadership camp they'd spent time together out in the woods, talking about really *important* things, listening to the water chattering in the brook, the

127

wind sighing in the trees. That had been a new experience for Daniel, and even though Lin was from D.C., whenever he thought of her he thought of the woods and the fresh, soft fragrances of that spot by the brook. Of course, the bad part of that was that whenever he saw a brook, he thought of Lin. Whenever he heard birds singing, he thought of Lin. Whenever —

He made himself stop. There was no point in going through the whole thing again. It was hopeless. With a sigh, he reached for the next set of papers. This one was a thick one, and he remembered that Torrey Easton had brought it in to the newspaper office at the same time he'd brought in the piece about biking. He looked at the corner of the first typed paper. Sara Gates. Oh, yeah, Daniel thought. That was the girl who had come up to him after his speech at the Holiday Inn. The pretty, bouncy blonde with all those bright ideas for a movie review column. Daniel smiled grimly. Everybody thought it was easy to write a review of a movie because all you had to say was that you liked it or you didn't like it. But it wasn't easy; it was really hard. It was one of the hardest kinds of newspaper writing that Daniel could think of because you had to know about the way movies were made and you had to be able to say what you knew without sounding pompous. And of course, you had to be interesting. The chances were better than even that Sara Gates had plenty of enthusiasm, but not much else.

But as Daniel read the first review, a short piece about *The Color Purple*, he sat up straighter

128

in his seat. This girl knew something about movies and moviemaking, that was for sure. She could read film characters the way you read characters in a book, and she seemed to understand what made them tick. And what's more, she could write. What a terrific combination!

Quickly, Daniel read through the other pieces Torrey Easton had brought in. Yes, there was no doubt about this one, absolutely no doubt. Sara Gates definitely had talent. Unless Daniel missed his guess, she had a better-than-average shot at doing this kind of thing for a living if she wanted to. And he'd be glad to give her a start in *The Red and the Gold*. With a flourish, he put her papers on the top of the "accept" pile. If he could land a couple more writers like Sara Gates, he'd have a *great* staff!

By noon, the "accept" pile had been topped off with two more submissions, and the rest had gone into the "reject" stack. Daniel sat back in his chair and stretched his legs. In the backyard, a squirrel scampered across the fence and up into a neighbor's maple tree, its tail flicking alertly. The squirrel's dark eyes were bright and shiny, and they watched the world with an avid curiosity that reminded him of . . . Daniel sighed and shook his head wearily. There they were again, thoughts of Lin pushing their way into his mind. He couldn't keep them out, no matter how hard he tried. And suddenly he didn't *want* to try anymore.

He looked at the phone on the wall. The last time he had called Lin's house, on a Sunday afternoon, he'd gotten her mother. But today was a weekday. Suppose he called today? Maybe he'd be able to actually talk to her. And anyway, he could hang up if somebody else answered the phone. Like her mother, for instance. He shivered at the thought of her mother's politely chilly voice. Yeah, he could always hang up.

He dialed quickly, his fingers shaking, before he could lose his nerve. The first time he misdialed and had to put the phone down and try again. Finally it began to ring, and Daniel twisted and untwisted the coiled cord around his finger, his insides clenched like a fist.

"Hello?"

Daniel felt the hard knot inside him beginning to melt as he heard Lin's sharp, intelligent voice. It was *her*! She sounded so real and immediate that he could actually shut his eyes and imagine her sitting there beside him, questioning him, making him see things he'd looked at for years but never really *seen*. Lin was the only girl in the world who could do that for him. That was why he couldn't let her go — not ever.

He swallowed. "Hello, Lin. It's Daniel."

There was a silence. Then Lin sighed. "Hello, Daniel," she said. Her voice sounded resigned.

Daniel hesitated. He wasn't sure he liked the tone of her voice. It sounded as if talking to him was something she hated to do but felt she had to. He took a deep breath. "Did your mother tell you I called?"

"Yes, she did," she said flatly. "I wish you hadn't."

"Lin," Daniel hurried on, before she could say more, "I know I really screwed things up for us. I made a mistake, a *bad* mistake. I moved too fast, before you'd had a chance to prepare your parents. I *know* all that. But I still think I deserve another chance." He stopped. "No," he said, more slowly, "that's not right. I think *we* deserve another chance. We're too good together. We can't just forget this relationship as if it were only an ordinary friendship. Because it's not. There's nothing ordinary about it. You've got to at least admit that."

There was a pause, and then Lin laughed, thinly. Her voice was brittle. "Yes," she said. "I have to admit that we haven't had an ordinary friendship."

"You see?" Daniel said triumphantly. And then he stopped. That was exactly the kind of stupid aggressiveness that had gotten him into trouble in the first place. "If it's not ordinary, then," he said, with more restraint, "it's got to be special. Right? Be honest."

Lin hesitated. "Yes, Daniel, our friendship has had its special qualities."

Daniel felt another surge of triumph. There! She'd admitted it! And Lin was a logical girl, the *most* logical girl he'd ever met. Surely if she had admitted this much, she would have to come to the same conclusion he'd come to weeks before. "Well, then," he said, still trying to sound reasonable and detached, "if our friendship is special, it's important — to both of us. And if it's important, we can't just end it, at least not without discussing it together. Lin, we *have* to see each other again. We just have to talk this out."

"Well, I — "

Daniel grinned to himself. She was considering it. Her voice was wavering, which meant she was torn.

"How could it hurt if we just got together and *talked*?" he asked insistently. "I mean, it's not as if we were going to run away and get married, is it? We'll just sit down and talk. We can even do it right out in public, if that's what you want."

"Well, maybe I. . . . " Her voice trailed away.

"I'll tell you what, Lin," Daniel said confidently. He knew that the triumph was showing in his voice, but he didn't care. She was going to say yes this time. He *knew* it. "I'll come to D.C. tomorrow. How about meeting me at the Lincoln Memorial about noon? We can go for a walk and — "

"No."

Daniel felt as if somebody had poked him with a sharp stick. He sucked in his breath. "You can't *mean* that, Lin."

"But I do," Lin said. This time there was no wavering in her voice, no hesitation. "I've made up my mind, Daniel, and I don't see any reason to change it, now or in the future. Things are over between us. It would be best if you stopped calling."

"But Lin — "

"Please, Daniel," Lin said, her voice as polite and frosty as her mother's had been. "Please stop calling. It's no use." There was a final, definite click as the phone went dead.

Daniel slammed down the phone. For a minute he sat there with his eyes shut, his fingers in his ears, trying to keep the sound of Lin's cold voice from echoing in his mind. Then he opened his eyes and reached for his red pen. Well, if he couldn't have Lin, there was plenty else to keep him busy. There was *The Red and the Gold*. He looked at the reject pile. While he was at it, he might as well give that punk Torrey Easton an idea of what he was up against. He pulled out Torrey's article and began to mark it up, viciously attacking the errors.

When he was finished, Torrey's paper looked like a battlefield, with bright red ink scrawled all over it.

Chapter *13*

Daniel's Friday afternoon meeting was being held in the newspaper office at Kennedy High. As Sara and Torrey went in, they noticed the building was almost empty and the lights were all off, with the exception of the lights in the principal's office, where the secretaries were working. Since the rain had begun again and the sky was gray, the halls were shadowed and gloomy. Their steps rang out eerily in the silence.

It's like coming back to school at night, Sara thought, when nobody else is there and you have the feeling that the empty halls are full of the ghosts of students from years past. She glanced at the lockers as they walked past them. So many of them had belonged to kids who had graduated and were now college freshmen. A crop of *new* seniors was taking their places.

Beside Sara, Torrey reached for her hand. "Spooky, isn't it?" he asked, with a little laugh.

"Yeah," Sara admitted. "I was just thinking of all the kids who won't be here this year. And then next year, *we'll* be seniors and worrying about what college we're going to. It really gives you something to think about."

It seemed almost like yesterday that she had walked down this very same hall on the way to her first class, intimidated by the older kids and the teachers, even a little scared, wondering what high school was going to be like. Well, things weren't a lot different now, when you got right down to it. She knew what high school was all about, and she'd discovered she could handle her classes without any difficulty. But now she had a *new* challenge — getting on the staff of *The Red and the Gold* — and that prospect was almost as scary as coming to high school in the first place.

"Well," Torrey said confidently, "I predict that you'll be so busy reviewing movies for the newspaper this year that you won't have time to worry about what's going to happen next year." He squeezed her hand.

"Do you really think so?" Sara asked nervously, glancing at him. "I know the Video Stop customers like my reviews, but they're not exactly experts." She shook her head. "I'm beginning to think maybe this is a waste of time."

"No way," Torrey told her. He grinned mischievously. "You'll make it. It's the old Easton intuition, you see? I've got this feeling that Daniel

135

Tackett is going to take one look at your writing and just fall all over himself to get you onto his staff. And when the Easton crystal ball clicks on" — he snapped his fingers — "you can bet your socks it's right."

Sara couldn't help grinning back, in spite of her nervousness about the upcoming meeting. One of the things that had been frustrating about Torrey was his constant anger. In class last year, he never seemed to be having fun, unless it was malicious fun. But now somehow she'd broken through his hard shell. Sara thought back to that morning, when he'd practically forced his way into her house and made her sit down and think about things she didn't want to think about. Really unpleasant things, things that troubled her so deeply that she spent most of her time trying to pretend they didn't exist. But by the end of the conversation, Torrey had made her laugh again, had given her a clearer perspective on her troubles.

"Hey," Torrey said, catching her elbow, "isn't this the place?" He gestured to a door that had a sign on it reading *The Red and the Gold*. Inside, Sara could hear the noisy sound of voices.

Sara nodded. "This is it." She glanced at Torrey, biting her lower lip. "You go in first."

Torrey looked down at her. "I tell you, Sara, you've got nothing to worry about," he said. "In fact, I'll even bet that Daniel decides to take *both* of us on. You can do a series on classic movies, and I'll do a series on classic bikes. You

136

know, 'The Bike That Ate Toledo,' 'The Bike That Went to the Moon,' 'The Bike — ' "

Giggling, Sara took a swipe at Torrey. He ducked and opened the door with a low bow. "After you," he said, and they went into the room together, still laughing.

The office of *The Red and the Gold* was crowded with kids sitting around tables, laughing and talking. Whenever Sara had come into this room before, the tables had been littered with layouts and page makeups. But now the tables were empty, and the bulletin boards — which were usually crowded with cut-sheets from the paper — were empty, too. An intelligent-looking girl with dark braids broke off her conversation when she saw Sara and smiled. "Hi, Sara," she called.

"Oh, hi, Melanie," Sara said. She gestured in the girl's direction. "How about sitting with them?" she asked Torrey. "Melanie was in one of my classes last year."

"Sure, if you like," Torrey said.

"Melanie, I'd like you to meet Torrey Easton," Sara said as they pulled out chairs and sat down. "Torrey, this is Melanie Herbert."

Melanie gave Torrey a cool look. "You're Roxanne Easton's brother, aren't you?"

Torrey nodded, his eyes narrowing. "Yeah," he said. He looked at her. "Do I know you?"

Melanie smiled. "Not really," she said. "I was doing some fill-in work at the *Rose Hill Bulletin* this summer, and I covered the accident you and your sister had in that Mercedes."

Sara looked at Torrey, concerned. "Accident?" she asked. "Were you in a car wreck? Were you hurt?"

A red flush crept up Torrey's neck. "No," he said, "I wasn't hurt." He looked away. It was obvious that it was something he didn't want to talk about. Feeling uncomfortable, Sara turned back to Melanie. "So, you're trying for a place on the newspaper staff, too?"

"I've submitted some gossip-column material," Melanie said with a toss of her head. "I don't think Daniel is very hot on gossip columns, but he has to know that a lot of kids only read *that* page of the newspaper." She gave Sara a curious look. "What about you?"

Sara smiled tentatively, trying to recapture some of the enthusiasm she usually felt when she was talking to somebody about her movie reviews. But try as she might, she couldn't summon up any of that bounce this afternoon. Most of what she was feeling was a kind of worried apprehension about whether her stuff was good enough for *The Red and the Gold*. "Oh," she said casually, "I sent in some movie reviews. Nothing spectacular, actually." Next to her, Torrey shifted in his chair.

Melanie arched her eyebrows. "Movie reviews?" she said. "Now *that's* something that ought to interest Daniel. I get the feeling he's out to improve his readers' minds, don't you?"

Before Sara could answer, another door opened and Daniel came in. His brown hair was falling across his eyes, as usual, and he was wearing jeans and boots. He dumped an armload of papers on the table at the front of the room and turned to face the students, brushing the hair out of his eyes with a quick, impatient gesture.

"Glad everybody could make it," he said in a gruff voice, looking around the room. "Thanks for taking the time to put your writing samples together. I've read them carefully" — he glanced at Torrey — "and I've written comments on most of them. I'd be happy to talk to you individually about your writing, but I thought first I'd let you ask any questions you might have." He looked around. "Is there anything you want to know about this year's newspaper?"

Next to Sara, Melanie raised her hand. "Are you going to keep the same columns that the newspaper has had in the past?" she asked.

Daniel folded his arms across his chest and regarded her thoughtfully. "For the most part, yes," he said. "We won't be ditching the student news column or the lead story, if that's what you're worried about. After all, we'd like to go on publishing instead of being strung up out in the middle of the quad." Laughter fluttered around the room. "I guess the biggest difference I'm hoping to make is in the quality of our news and feature coverage and the quality of the writing," he went on. "That's why I want to be sure that we recruit the very best writers at Kennedy High."

Melanie sat back, satisfied, but Sara felt her stomach tighten. The very best writers. She knew she was good, but was she one of the very best? It didn't seem likely, and she began to be sorry that she'd ever gotten the idea of trying out for the staff. She felt a sour taste in her mouth. If Daniel was going to recruit only the very best, she'd better get prepared for a rejection.

"Any other questions?" Daniel looked around the room. "Okay. I'd like to talk to the following people first." He read off a list of about seven or eight names. Sara shut her eyes. Torrey's name was on the list, but hers wasn't. Were those the people who had made the staff or not? "If you'll come up to this table one at a time," Daniel went on, "I'll discuss your submissions with you." He waved his hand. "I guess the rest of you can just sort of hang around until I can get to you. Word has it that the soda machine has been filled up already, if anybody's thirsty."

Somebody shouted, "Are you buying, Daniel?" and everybody laughed. Chairs scraped, people began to gather in small groups. The kids whose names Daniel had called went toward the front of the room.

"Good luck," Sara said, and she gave Torrey's hand a squeeze.

He shrugged. "It doesn't mean all that much to me," he said carelessly. "The only reason I want to get on the paper is so we can be together."

Impulsively, Sara stood on tiptoe and gave him a quick kiss on the cheek. "Thanks," she whispered and pushed him toward the front of the room.

"How about a soda?" Melanie asked, and the two girls left the room together. She glanced back over her shoulder. "I want to hear what you've been doing all summer."

When they came back, five minutes later, Sara saw that Torrey was standing beside Daniel, listening to him and looking down at a paper on the table. His face wore a tight, sullen look.

Uh-oh, Sara thought with a shiver. She said, "see you," to Melanie and went to stand by the door, waiting for Torrey. After a moment, Daniel handed him the paper, saying something that Sara couldn't hear. Torrey turned on his heel and stamped to the door.

"What happened?" Sara asked anxiously, catching him by the sleeve.

"He didn't like it, *that's* what happened," Torrey said in a grim voice. He threw a furious glance back over his shoulder. "He told me that if I'm interested in writing for the paper, I ought to learn how to spell first." His mouth twisted into a sarcastic grin, and he began to mimic Daniel's voice. "Learn your ABCs, kid, and *then* I'll think about giving you a job." He wadded up the paper he held in his hand and threw it on the floor.

Sara laughed lightly, trying to nudge Torrey out of his angry mood. "Is spelling your only problem? Well, that's easy enough to fix." She put her hand on his arm and smiled up at him, encouraging him to loosen up. "You can get better at that with just a little practice."

Torrey glared at her. "*You* can practice spelling if you want to," he fumed. His voice was rising, and Sara had the uncomfortable feeling that the others were looking at them. "I'm not interested in stupid things like that." He paused and stared in Daniel's direction, looking as if he wanted to be sure he was heard. "I'm not interested in working for a stupid rag that's only good for wrapping the garbage. I've got better things to do with my time."

"But Torrey, I thought you said — " Sara began helplessly, feeling almost paralyzed by his anger.

"*Forget* what I said!" Torrey jerked away from her hand. "And forget about *me*, too." As he left the room, he slammed the door behind him so hard that the glass rattled.

At the desk, Daniel looked up. "Sara Gates?" he said, reading from a list in his hand. "Sara, are you still here? I'd like to talk to you, please."

Sara looked at the door, torn between going after Torrey and finding out what Daniel had thought of her work. But her instinct told her that there wasn't really any point in trying to talk to Torrey when he was feeling this way. She knew what it was like to be that angry — those moods came on her, too — and it would probably be better to leave him alone for a while and try to talk it over later, when he had cooled down a little. Quickly, she bent over and picked up the wadded-up paper that Torrey had thrown on the floor. Then she turned and walked to the desk at the front of the room.

"I'm Sara Gates," she said, still thinking about Torrey.

Daniel looked up at her and brushed the hair out of his face. "Yeah," he said, "I remember. You came up to talk to me after my speech at the Rotary Club meeting." He put his hand on the sheaf of papers on the desk. "Looks like we've got a winner here," he said.

"A what?" Sara asked. "A — a winner?"

Daniel grinned. "I think you have a lot of potential as a writer. And I think that *The Red and the Gold* will be very fortunate if you'll agree to join the staff as its first film reviewer."

Sara stared at him, only half believing what he'd said. "You mean you liked my stuff?"

"Liked it?" Daniel asked. He laughed softly "Yeah, I liked it. If I were editing it, you know what I'd do with it?"

Sara bit her lip. "No, what?" she asked.

"I'd do absolutely nothing," Daniel said flatly. "That's how good it is." He picked up her reviews and put them back into a big manila envelope. "I'm not saying that you don't have a lot to learn or a lot of hard work ahead of you. As time goes on, you're going to get better. But I am saying that you're ahead of the game already. Welcome aboard, Sara." He held out the envelope. "I'll tell our advisor to expect you to sign up for journalism, okay?"

Sara took the envelope, feeling breathless. "Yes," she said. "And thanks. Thanks a lot."

"Don't thank me," Daniel said. "You're the one who wrote that good stuff." He gave her a narrow look. "Is Torrey Easton a friend of yours?"

Sara nodded. "Yes, he is," she said, meeting Daniel's eyes.

Daniel glanced down and began to shuffle through some other papers on his desk. "I guess maybe I went a little overboard when I marked up his work," he said slowly. "I didn't mean to make him mad. It's just that . . . well, something came up when I was looking at his stuff, and I — " He stopped and then started again. "I probably overdid it a little. I mean, his writing still needs a lot of improvement before he's ready to join a newspaper, but his work wasn't as bad as I made it sound. Will you tell him that maybe he ought to take another shot at it?"

Sara sighed. "Yeah," she said. "I'll tell him."

The Eastons' town house was quiet and dark when Sara came up the front steps. It didn't look like anybody was at home, and she wasn't surprised when nobody answered the doorbell. After a minute or two, she rummaged in her purse for a pencil. Then she took Torrey's wadded-up paper out of her purse and smoothed it out, thinking. On the way over, she'd read what he had written, and it had brought tears to her eyes. Oh, sure, Daniel was right — there *were* a lot of spelling and grammatical errors. But the heart of the article, its *soul*, was what had spoken to her, and she'd known exactly what Torrey was trying to say about biking and the way he felt when he was out riding all by himself. His writing had communicated to her, and *that* was what good writing was all about, wasn't it? Anybody could spell and put commas in the right places, but not everybody could communicate real feelings the way Torrey had.

She turned the paper over and began to write on the back:

Dear Torrey,

I've read your piece and I think it's wonderful, even if there are some spelling problems. I know you're disappointed about the way Daniel reacted. But do you remember what you told me this morning, about not giving up? About being brave enough to face disappointments? Please, think about it. I'll wait for you outside the journalism class on the first day of school. I believe in you. And I love you.

Sara

She put the paper into the manila envelope that had held her reviews and licked the flap to seal it shut. On the outside she wrote Torrey's name, and then she put it into the Easton's mailbox. She turned with a sigh. There wasn't anything she could do now except hope.

Chapter
14

Looking up at the clear sky, Charlotte smiled. She and Roxanne had just pulled into the huge, sprawling parking lot of the Maryland State Fair Grounds. It had drizzled for the past couple of days, and she'd had her fingers crossed. It *couldn't* rain — not for their last party of the summer!

The girls got out of the car and wove their way through the lot toward the entrance gate. It was nearly noon, the time they were supposed to meet the others. Charlotte glanced at Roxanne, who was wearing a skimpy red mini and a cropped yellow top.

"Aren't you afraid you're going to get sunburned?" she asked. Charlotte had worn white pants and a pink top with long sleeves, and she'd pulled her blonde hair back from her face with a pink ribbon.

Roxanne grinned and smoothed her skirt. "I never burn, I *tan*," she said airily. "Oh, there they are!" she exclaimed a moment later. "Look, there are Jonathan and Lily, with Greg. And there's Vince!"

Charlotte winced. On the way over, Roxanne had talked about nothing but Vince. To hear her tell it, they had completely made up their differences that night at the Holiday Inn, and their relationship was back on the right track again, exactly the way it used to be. But Charlotte knew that Vince would never have asked her out if he was still going out with Roxanne. Roxanne must be mistaken. But how could she deceive herself this way? Charlotte wondered. It was a mystery — a complete mystery.

"Hi, Charlotte!" Lily said, with the others right behind her. Vince was standing with them, too, lounging with his back to the fence, his hands in his pockets. Charlotte's heart did a quick flip when she saw him. His dark eyes met hers and held them for an instant, and then she tore her glance away, her pulse racing.

"Hi, Lily," Charlotte said. She turned to smile at Jonathan, hoping her confusion didn't show. "I thought you'd be off at Penn by now."

"Not quite yet," Jonathan answered with a grin at Lily. She was half-turned away, saying something to Daniel, who had just walked up. Jonathan was holding Lily's hand the way a drowning man holds onto a piece of wood. "I've had a few last-minute things to do," he said. *"Important* things."

Beside Charlotte, Roxanne was leaning toward Vince. "Hi, Vince," she said in a soft, breathy voice. "It's so good to see you." Charlotte felt a quick shock of surprise. She hadn't heard Roxanne use that voice in a long while. It was her "sexy" voice.

Vince looked at Roxanne. "Hi, Roxanne," he said in a casual tone. Then he glanced up. "Hey, here come Stacy and Zack. And Frankie and Josh are with them."

"So what does everyone want to do first?" Charlotte asked after they had all greeted one another.

"I vote for the Ferris wheel," Frankie offered in her quiet way. "I mean, that'll give us a good view of the fairgrounds, and we can decide from there what we want to do."

Josh put his arm around her shoulders. "Are you sure?" he teased. "The last time we went on a Ferris wheel, you covered your eyes. How can you see what's going on with your eyes covered?"

Roxanne threw a seductive glance at Vince. "I vote for the bumper cars," she said. "And maybe we should split up, instead of staying together. That way we can do whatever we want."

"But the idea was to have a farewell-to-summer party," Zack objected. "How can we have a party if we split up?"

Charlotte didn't think much of Roxanne's idea, but she didn't want to say so. "Why don't we go in and get a hot dog or something," she suggested. "We can decide what we're going to do while we're eating."

"Now *that's* a great idea," Zack said, sounding suddenly enthusiastic. "Let's scope out the hot dogs." He looked surprised when everybody laughed.

"That's Zack for you," Josh said. "Always thinking about food."

As they all trooped in through the gate, Roxanne tossed her head. Charlotte's idea about having something to eat was okay — it would give her a few minutes to decide exactly how to get close to Vince. She shivered deliciously, imagining how it would feel to have Vince's arm around her as they crowded into one of those little bumper cars. They always threw you into your partner's lap, she thought happily. Yes, the thing she had to do now was to get *close* to Vince.

They all gathered noisily around the nearest food stand and ordered hot dogs with all the trimmings. After they had eaten, they cruised the fairgrounds, having a terrific time gawking at the livestock entries, laughing at the antics of the clowns and trained monkeys, and browsing in front of the crafts booths.

Roxanne, still thinking about the exciting possibility of riding in the bumper cars with Vince, was sticking as close to him as she could. Still, there was something she didn't quite understand, and it nibbled annoyingly at her confidence. There always seemed to be somebody standing or walking *between* her and Vince, wherever they were. If she didn't know better, she might think he was doing it on purpose. As it was, she had to keep a careful eye out for a chance to be alone with him. When they came to the Ferris wheel, she stepped up beside him, catching him unaware.

"Oh, let's ride the Ferris wheel," she cried, putting her hand on his arm and flashing him the smile that always melted the other guys she'd known.

Vince looked like he was about to shake his head. Then he caught Charlotte's eye. "Tell you what," he said, "there's room in the seat for three. How about if we all ride together?"

For a second, Roxanne hesitated. What was going on between Vince and Charlotte? But then she pushed the question to the back of her mind. He must have invited Charlotte so that she wouldn't feel left out. Rox caught Vince's hand, pulling him forward. "Terrific!" she exclaimed. "Let's go!" If there were three of them, they'd have to sit that much closer together, wouldn't they?

So they rode the Ferris wheel, with Vince in the middle, between Roxanne and Charlotte. But Roxanne wasn't even conscious of Charlotte's presence. Vince had put his arm across the back of the seat and she could feel the roughness of his shirt against the thin fabric of her top. She closed her eyes and relaxed against him, pressing her body against his. This intimacy was exactly what they needed to bring them together again, she thought happily, exactly what they needed to renew their bond before the hectic first days of school. For the first time since their breakup, she

150

was *certain* that things were going to be all right between them.

On the other side of Vince, Charlotte sat holding herself rigidly, as far away from Vince as she could. He had put his arm on the back of the seat, just gently touching her shoulders. It was a meaningless gesture, the same kind of gesture that Josh or Zack would make, without any kind of suggestive overtone. But Charlotte couldn't help shivering — and not from the cool breeze that gently rocked their seat. It was Vince's touch that made her shiver, and as she admitted that fact to herself she also had to admit something else. As the Ferris wheel swooped and circled, lifting them high and then dropping them down toward the ground again, she had to admit that she was falling for Vince, falling headlong and out of control. It was the most frightening feeling she'd ever had in her whole life. And she didn't know what to do about it.

When the ride was over and they had all climbed off the Ferris wheel, Stacy pointed to a dance floor nearby where a group of musicians in cowboy garb were just beginning to play. "Hey, it's a square dance!" she exclaimed, and grabbed Zack, hauling him toward the dance floor.

Laughing and shouting, the rest followed, and in a few minutes they were all on the floor, carrying out the caller's instructions. At first, Charlotte felt a sharp sense of relief, glad to be away from Vince's disturbing physical presence. She was paired with Greg, who flashed his friendly smile at her and whirled her around in a brotherly bear-hug. But the trouble started when they had to change partners in the dance, and every few minutes she found herself do-si-do-ing with Vince, turned, and guided by *his* strong arms. Charlotte sucked in a deep breath, trying to avoid his direct, warm glance as they dipped and turned in the dance. But it was hard, because *his* eyes were fastened on hers, and she could see an intense, searching look in them that made her even more breathless. The dance took her away for a moment, back into Greg's arms. But just when she'd gotten herself together and controlled her feelings, she was pulled back to Vince again, as if by some mysterious, magnetic force. Pulled back to the thrill of his touch and the intense look in his eyes that made her heart pound and her knees feel weak. The worst of it was that her willpower felt even weaker than her knees, and with every moment that passed, she lost more of her resolve to resist him.

Finally, at the end of the second dance, Charlotte couldn't stand it anymore. She had to get away from Vince, from the almost magnetic attraction of his eyes. "Hey, everybody," she said shakily, "there's too much going on here to spend the whole afternoon square dancing. Let's go look for something else to do."

"What's the matter, Charlotte?" Zack teased. "Can't you take the action?"

Charlotte stared at him. Had he seen what was going on between her and Vince? If Zack — who was inclined to be a bit slow about things like

152

that — had noticed, *Roxanne* had probably noticed, too! Then it dawned on her that he was talking about the strenuous exercise of the square dance, and she laughed along with the others.

"I know what we can do," Lily said. "There's a band playing over there, past the pizza booth. Let's go listen!"

Everyone agreed happily, and they all followed Lily, who found a place for them right in front of the stage. There was room to dance, and soon Lily and Jonathan were dancing and clapping in time to the music. Lily loved to dance, and this afternoon, with the warm sun on her shoulders and the strong, rhythmic beat of the music pounding around her, she danced with an abandon that she seldom permitted herself. In fact, she was so wrapped up in the music, so lost in it, that she almost forgot that Jonathan was dancing with her. It was almost like dancing alone.

Suddenly the lead singer, a good-looking blond guy, leaned over and pulled her up on stage. "Come on, little girl, let's dance," he said, and without even thinking about it, without thinking at all, Lily kept on moving, swaying with the rhythm, letting her hips move the way they felt like moving, tossing her head, and snapping her fingers. It was like being in a dream, dancing up there in front of the crowd, just like the girl in the old Bruce Springsteen video. And it was still almost a dream, when at the end of the song, the lead singer playfully wrapped his arms around her and gave her a big kiss.

153

"Hey, you're something *else*," he said admiringly, and then let her go.

Back on the ground, in front of the stage, Lily woke up again. Roxanne and Stacy were there, talking. "Wow, was that for *real*?" Stacy asked, impressed. "What a kick!" Roxanne looked envious. "How'd you get him to let you up there?" she asked.

But Jonathan wasn't impressed *or* envious — just miserable. He pulled her over to the side of the crowd, behind the musicians' van, and wrapped his arms around her tightly. "I can't take this, Lily," he groaned, burying his face in her neck. "I just can't take it."

"But I wasn't doing anything, Jonathan," Lily said, trying to push him away so she could make him look at her. "I was just dancing, that's all!"

"I know," Jonathan said tonelessly. "But whenever I see you with somebody else — whether you're talking or dancing or whatever — I get this sick feeling inside me." He pulled back a fraction and looked down at her, his eyes searching. "Listen, I've got to ask you this, Lily. And you've got to say yes."

Lily sucked in her breath. Behind them the music was still pounding, louder and louder. "Say yes to what?"

"Say that you won't see any other guys while I'm away at college."

Lily closed her eyes. Ever since that day on the beach, she'd known this question was coming. But even though she'd thought about it and thought about it, she still wasn't sure she could

154

give him the answer he wanted. How could she say yes? It was a promise that she suspected she couldn't keep. And yet Jonathan was holding her so tightly she could hardly breathe, pleading with his eyes, with his heart and soul. How could she say no?

"Please, Lily," Jonathan said, the sound of heartbreak in his voice. "I love you!" He bent his head to hers and kissed her. His lips tasted salty with tears. For a brief moment, Lily tried to pull away from him, but his arms tightened and he began to kiss her, very hard.

After a moment he let her go. Lily opened her eyes. She knew their relationship was more important to Jonathan just now than anything else. If she let him go off to college feeling unsure and uncertain about how things were between them, it might seriously damage his chances for success. And anyway, once he was away at Penn, he'd probably be so busy with his new friends that he'd stop feeling so anxious and possessive about her.

She looked at him. "If that's what you truly want, Jonathan," she said, slowly and reluctantly, "I'll promise. I won't date anybody else while you're away."

Jonathan put his fingers under her chin and tilted her face up to his. "Oh, Lily," he whispered, "it *is* what I want. And it's wonderful to know that you want it, too!" He kissed her again.

The noise of the music followed Charlotte as she made her way through the crowd, on her way

155

to the soda stand. The others were still listening to the band. Charlotte shook her head. As far as she was concerned, a little rock music went a long way, especially *loud* rock.

"Pretty hard on the eardrums, huh?" It was Vince, standing in her way.

Charlotte looked up, startled. "Oh, yes, I guess it is," she said. "I thought I'd get something to drink."

"I know," Vince said. "I saw you leave." He stepped toward her, his eyes dark. She couldn't pull her eyes away, couldn't stop looking at him. "How about if I go with you."

Charlotte hesitated. She should say no. But Vince was so close he made her feel breathless, shaky. She didn't really have the *strength* to say no. Finally, she managed a nod.

Vince fell into step beside her as they walked across the fairgrounds, cutting behind the tents on their way to the food concessions. After a moment, Charlotte felt him take her hand, curling his fingers around hers. And then he turned her to face him.

"Char," he said, looking seriously at her, "are you feeling the same things I'm feeling?"

Somewhere nearby a calliope was playing loudly, and Charlotte could hear children shouting. But then the sounds began to fade away, and it seemed to her as if there was nothing else in the world but the two of them. She took a deep breath. "I think so," she whispered.

And then he stepped closer and slipped his

arms around her. Soon he was kissing her as if he couldn't help himself.

For an instant, Charlotte felt herself melting into Vince's arms, feeling his lips gently touching hers, giving herself up to the strength of his embrace. The whole world seemed to dip and whirl around them until she was giddy and light-headed with the intensity of the emotion that welled up inside her. But then she pulled back, suddenly remembering.

"Stop, Vince," she said urgently, breathlessly. She put her finger to his lips. "Stop, please!"

Reluctantly, Vince let her go. "Don't you feel it, too?" he asked in a low voice. "*I* do, Charlotte. I know you must."

Charlotte tried to steady herself. "It doesn't matter what I feel," she said. "All that matters is that Roxanne is my friend, and I can't hurt her. I can't get involved with you now."

"But I don't understand," Vince said, a look of total confusion on his face. "I've already told Roxanne that everything's over between us. I would never have called you the other day if I hadn't set things straight with Roxanne."

Charlotte bit her lip. She could hear the honesty in Vince's voice. It was one of the things about him that she . . . that she *loved*.

"I know, Vince," she said, amazed as she heard herself speaking in what sounded like such a reasonable, *logical* tone of voice, when she really felt like crying. It was almost as if the words were being spoken by somebody else. "And I believe you when you say that you've ended it with Roxanne. But I've also got to look at this from her point of view. Your feelings toward her may have changed, but she's still crazy about you. And as long as she feels that way, you and I can't be together. Don't you see?"

Vince looked at her for a long moment, the pain clear and sharp in his eyes. "Yes, I see," he said. "You're so honest and good that you won't hurt a friend, even a friend who is living in the past." He shook his head with a sad little laugh. "It makes me even more sure that I love you. *You're* the one I want, Charlotte. You're the one I need."

Charlotte tried to swallow the huge lump that was burning in her throat. "I feel the same way," she whispered, "but it can't be." She was blinking back tears, the logic and reason crumbling under the feelings that pounded at her. "I—I have to go now." She had to get away from him before she broke down and cried.

"Please don't," Vince said, his voice ragged. "Please don't go!"

"But I *have* to, Vince," she said. "We really can't see each other anymore."

With a sad sigh, he nodded, then folded her to him and kissed her. And then he pulled away again and faded into the crowd. But Charlotte didn't see him go. Her eyes were too full of tears.

Chapter
15

The halls of Kennedy High were filled with mobs of shouting kids, searching for their new lockers with their arms full of books, exchanging stories of summer adventures, trying to figure out their new class schedules. Sara Gates stood outside of the journalism classroom, watching the crowds swirl past, a frown on her face and her fingers crossed. It was almost time for class to begin, and the questions chased each other around madly in her mind. Was Torrey coming to journalism class? Had her note to him made him understand how much she cared — or had it made him even more angry about the way things had turned out?

With a sinking heart, Sara glanced at her watch. He *wasn't* coming. Her efforts had failed. But just at that moment, she heard a shout.

"Sara! Hey, Sara, wait a minute!" It was Torrey, racing through the crowd.

"Oh, Torrey!" Sara exclaimed happily. "I'm so *glad* to see you!"

Torrey put his hand on her shoulder and his eyes met hers. "I got your note," he said, then added meaningfully, "Thanks."

Sara wasn't sure what to say. She took a deep breath. "What did you decide?" she asked. "About your article, I mean?"

Torrey flipped open his notebook and pulled out a paper. "I've rewritten it," he said, "and I want you to give it to Daniel. But I'm not taking journalism."

"You're not?" Sara felt a wave of disappointment flood through her.

Torrey shook his head. "I thought about it, and I realized that I'm not really interested in journalism. I did the story for *you*. But I've changed my study hall elective — to mechanics. One of the guys told me that you learn some stuff about bicycles in that class. So that's where I'm headed." He looked at this watch. "I don't want to be late. I have the feeling that this is one class I might really get into."

Sara smiled. "Oh, Torrey that's great!" she exclaimed.

He grinned. "*You're* great," he said. Quickly he bent forward and kissed her. "Listen, I'm really sorry for being such a jerk at the newspaper meeting. I don't know what got into me, blowing up like that at you. You didn't have anything to do with what happened, and I didn't have any right to take my feelings out on you."

Sara smoothed his cheek with her finger. "It's okay, really," she said softly, touched by his apology. "We've both got a lot of things to work through, and emotions are going to come boiling up sometimes when we aren't ready to cope with them."

"Yeah," Torrey said. "You're probably right. I hope you'll stick with me, even through those times." His eyes searched hers. "Will you, Sara? I have the feeling that if we're together, we'll both be all right."

Wordlessly, Sara nodded. Her heart was too full to speak.

"Hey, Roxanne!" Charlotte dodged through the crowded hallway toward Roxanne's locker, ducking under a paper airplane that came zipping out of one of the classrooms and skirting a group of jabbering freshman girls gathered around the drinking fountain. "How are you this morning?" she asked happily. "Isn't this a great day? I *love* the first day of school. Even though I had my outfit all planned out weeks ahead of time, I changed my mind fifteen times while I was getting ready. I finally decided on this blue skirt and blouse. What do you think?"

Roxanne turned to face her. "Good morning, Charlotte," she responded, coolly and distinctly, her green eyes on Charlotte's. "Yes, I like your outfit. It's very attractive, as usual."

Charlotte put out a friendly hand to touch Roxanne's arm, but Roxanne pulled back. "What's the matter, Rox?" Charlotte asked sympathetically. "Are you still feeling feverish?"

On the way back from the fair the day before, Roxanne had been uncharacteristically silent, and when Charlotte had asked her what was the matter, she'd said that she'd gotten a headache from all the running around. Her face was still flushed this morning under her makeup, Charlotte noticed, and she held her shoulders with an unnatural, almost wooden stiffness, as if it hurt to move.

Roxanne nodded and opened her locker. "I'll be fine," she said tonelessly.

"Well, I hope you get better," Charlotte said in a soothing voice. "There are so many exciting things going on this week, with classes getting started and everything. I'd hate for you to miss any part of it."

Roxanne gave her a peculiar look. "I'm sure things *will* get better," she said. "I have a remedy or two in mind." She turned and began to stack her books onto the top shelf of her locker.

After a second, Charlotte continued, feeling a little puzzled by Roxanne's silence. "This morning, when I got to advisory, I found out that the senior class has a new faculty advisor. Her name is Mrs. Wilson, and she's just transferred here from D.C. I've already met her. She's got some great ideas for class activities. I can't wait to talk to you about them and find out what you think."

"I'll just bet you can't," Roxanne said softly,

putting the last book on the shelf. She looked into the little mirror that was glued to the door and began to brush her hair, turning her back on Charlotte.

Charlotte frowned. "Roxanne, are you *sure* everything's all right?" she asked worriedly. "I mean, you're acting awfully strange this morning. Is there something you want to talk about?"

Roxanne kept on brushing her hair. "I'm fine," she said, clipping her words. "And there's nothing for us to talk about. Nothing at all."

"Well, then, shouldn't we be on our way to lunch?" Charlotte asked, glancing at her watch. "I want to ask everybody what they think about maybe getting together one day after school to — "

"If you're so anxious to see everyone," Roxanne broke in, still brushing her hair, "why don't you just go on? I'll be there in a few minutes. I have something to do first."

"Are you sure?" Charlotte asked. "I mean, I don't mind waiting for you."

"I'm sure."

"Well, then," Charlotte said happily, "I think I will just go on. Everybody's probably out on the quad by now, in our regular place. I'll save you a spot, okay?"

Roxanne tossed her hair and put her brush into her purse. "Okay," she said.

With a little wave, Charlotte turned to go, and Roxanne watched her disappear around the corner. Her face tightened into a mask of pain and anger.

The memory of yesterday afternoon sliced through Roxanne like a dull knife, tearing at her insides. The crowd had still been listening to the rock band when Roxanne had seen Charlotte slip away from the group. For a minute, Roxanne had just dismissed it. Charlotte was probably going to get a soft drink or something. But then, out of the corner of her eye, she had seen Vince follow Charlotte, quietly, as if he didn't want anybody to notice that he was leaving. And at that moment, with a sudden flash of insight, she had remembered. Remembered the strange look that Vince had given Charlotte on the Ferris wheel. For a second, Roxanne hadn't been able to move, almost gasping for breath. There was something going on between Vince and Charlotte! Something they didn't want anybody else to know about!

Making sure that no one noticed, Roxanne had left the crowd, keeping Vince's tall, solid figure in sight as he made his way through the noisy fairgrounds. They hadn't gone very far when Vince caught up with Charlotte. The two of them had talked for a moment, and then — Roxanne's heart twisted inside her when she thought about it — he had kissed her, hard and passionately. They had pulled apart and Charlotte had put her fingers gently to his lips, probably warning him that they shouldn't be seen kissing in public. Then they talked for a moment more, no doubt planning their next secret meeting, and then there had been another kiss. It was a tender, lingering kiss that seemed to Roxanne as if it would never end. And after a while, Charlotte and Vince had both come back to the crowd and joined in the fun, a little flushed and breathless, but acting as if nothing at all had happened.

Standing in the hallway, oblivious to the noise and confusion of sixth-period lunch-hour traffic, Roxanne clenched her hands into tight fists. In her wildest dreams, she would never have imagined that Charlotte — sweet, friendly, superwarm Charlotte — would stoop to stealing her boyfriend away from her. And there was no doubt about it — it *was* stealing! It had taken a while, but she and Vince had made up their differences. They'd gotten back together again, and everything was going to be just the way it had been in the past. But now, with Charlotte in the picture, everything was changed. Roxanne bit her lip until she could practically taste blood in her mouth. She couldn't imagine a friend doing anything worse than what Charlotte had done to her. It was like a knife in her back.

Roxanne slowly turned her back to her locker and shut the door. A determination was growing within her, a hard, cold, unyielding determination. She would pay Charlotte back for taking Vince away from her. She didn't know how she would do it, or where, or when. But she *would* do it. And when she did, Charlotte DeVries would feel the deep, unspeakable pain that wrenched Roxanne at this very moment. Yes, retribution. That was the only thing that could soothe the pain of losing Vince. That was the only thing that would satisfy her.

Straightening her shoulders, Roxanne went down the hall toward the cafeteria and the quad, where the crowd was waiting.

Coming soon . . .
Couples #36
HOLD ME TIGHT

By the time Mrs. Weiss called her name, Lily was pumped to audition, the adrenaline making her toes and fingers tingle. Right now, nothing existed for Lily beyond the stage and the script.

At the end of the scene, two pink spots of exertion on her pale cheeks, Lily looked to Mrs. Weiss for direction. There was a sparkle of approval in her eyes. Mrs. Weiss waved the next auditioner up and Lily trotted down the steps, hardly feeling her feet on the scuffed wooden boards. She was exhilarated from the audition and from the knowledge that she'd done well. She wished there was someone waiting for her in the audience — Jonathan, or one of her girlfriends — anyone to share her excitement with. Oh well, Lily thought carelessly, taking the next stair with an extra bounce.

Then all at once she noticed there *was* some-one waiting for her, kind of. As she reached the bottom step, Lily found herself looking straight into Buford Wodjovodski's sky-blue eyes. Lily froze, her limbs suddenly feeling like they were made of marble. Buford's eyes found hers and his face broke into a smile. Unthinkingly, Lily smiled back with equal warmth. For the long moment that Buford held her gaze, they might as well have been the only two people in the theater.

Don't miss any exciting adventures of the popular Cheerleaders of Tarenton High!

☐ 41034-2	#1	**TRYING OUT** Caroline B. Cooney	$2.50
☐ 41531-X	#2	**GETTING EVEN** Christopher Pike	$2.50
☐ 33404-2	#3	**RUMORS** Caroline B. Cooney	$2.25
☐ 33405-0	#4	**FEUDING** Lisa Norby	$2.25
☐ 41437-2	#5	**ALL THE WAY** Caroline B. Cooney	$2.50
☐ 40840-2	#6	**SPLITTING** Jennifer Sarasin	$2.50
☐ 40371-0	#23	**PROVING IT** Diane Hoh	$2.50
☐ 40341-9	#24	**GOING STRONG** Super Edition Carol Ellis	$2.95
☐ 40446-6	#25	**STEALING SECRETS** Ann E. Steinke	$2.50
☐ 40447-4	#26	**TAKING OVER** Jennifer Sarasin	$2.50
☐ 40505-5	#27	**SPRING FEVER** Super Edition Diane Hoh	$2.95
☐ 40633-7	#28	**SCHEMING** Lisa Norby	$2.50
☐ 40634-5	#29	**FALLING IN LOVE** Ann E. Steinke	$2.50
☐ 40635-3	#30	**SAYING YES** Caroline B. Cooney	$2.50
☐ 40636-1	#31	**SHOWING OFF** Carol Ellis	$2.50
☐ 40637-X	#32	**TOGETHER AGAIN** Super Edition Jennifer Sarasin	$2.95
☐ 41010-5	#33	**SAYING NO** Ann E. Steinke	$2.50
☐ 40999-9	#34	**COMING BACK** Lisa Norby	$2.50
☐ 41011-3	#35	**MOVING UP** Leslie Davis	$2.50
☐ 41162-4	#36	**CHANGING LOVES** Judith Weber	$2.50

Complete series available wherever you buy books.
